LYNN FLORKIEWICZ

◆

LORD JAMES HARRINGTON AND THE AUTUMN MYSTERY

Complete and Unabridged

LINFORD
Leicester

First published in Great Britain

First Linford Edition
published 2018

Copyright © 2014 by Lynn Florkiewicz
All rights reserved

This book is a work of fiction. Names, characters, places and incidents are the product of the
author's imagination or used fictitiously. Any
resemblance to actual events, locales, or persons,
living or dead, is coincidental.

A catalogue record for this book is available
from the British Library.

ISBN 978–1–4448–3888–6

Published by
F. A. Thorpe (Publishing)
Anstey, Leicestershire

Set by Words & Graphics Ltd.
Anstey, Leicestershire
Printed and bound in Great Britain by
T. J. International Ltd., Padstow, Cornwall

This book is printed on acid-free paper

I'm dedicating this Autumn Mystery to those people who have supported me from the first book in the series. As some of you know, writing is my hobby; I discovered writing after a particularly debilitating illness and began these novels strictly for fun and recuperation. My plan was to write four seasonal mysteries and stop.

However, I never envisaged such a great following and due to the fantastic feedback from many of you along with some wonderful reviews, I've decided to carry on. Lord James Harrington and the Christmas Mystery will be next in the series.

1

Early August 1958

Cory House, an imposing property standing in its own grounds at the edge of Cavendish, had a forlorn look about it; it was in a state of sad neglect. Decaying leaves blew across a gravel drive which was beginning to surrender itself to weeds and tufts of grass. Overgrown shrubs encroached on the broad lawn and untamed trees reached out in all directions, shielding the residence from the main road. A rusty Ford Anglia was parked by the side wall near a dented metal dustbin.

In the far corner of the grounds was a pile of rubbish and, beyond that, a ramshackle fence. A solitary crow cawed in the distance.

Christie Cameron, a wiry sixty-year-old with a pasty complexion and a world-weary scowl, stood in the doorway and watched the removal van trundle down the drive. He turned. An echo boomed down the tiled hallway as he slammed the huge oak door shut. Half a dozen tea chests, some opened, lined the entrance from the front door to the kitchen at the rear of the property. He kept an eye on his elder sister, Jeannie, as she retrieved crockery from one, discarding its temporary newspaper wrapping.

'Jeannie?' he shouted in an abrasive Glaswegian accent. 'Tea in the front room.'

He watched as she placed the plates on the kitchen table, smoothed down her apron and with a pinched expression acknowledged the order in a thin voice.

'It's made, brother dear,' she said in a clipped Scottish tone. 'Sit by the fire. I've stoked it.' She rubbed her arms. 'It'll take time to warm these rooms. They've been empty for too long.' She looked at the ceiling. 'The gas fire is heating the room upstairs.'

Christie shoved his hands in the pockets of his threadbare cardigan. 'You've no business up there till dinner.'

Lips pursed, she boiled the kettle as Christie shuffled into the front room and straightened the wooden cross above the fireplace. Flames laboured around the logs as the fire in the grate struggled to take hold. With a puff of his cheeks, he eased himself down into an old fireside chair, rested his hand on the family bible and closed his eyes. The rattle of china interrupted the silence. Jeannie came in and placed a cup of strong tea on a small table to the side of him.

'It's a damp house, brother. The grates are lit in the rooms downstairs.'

Christie's rheumy eyes gazed at the flickering flame. Jeannie perched on the edge of a similar chair, upright and formal, her greying hair pulled back to form a tight bun.

'You'll be at peace here, brother.'

He took a breath and exhaled loudly. 'Aye, sister,' he said, casting an eye to the ceiling. 'You've locked the door?'

'Always, brother.' With a nod to the bible she asked: 'Shall we pray?'

'Aye.' He tightened his grip on the book.

2

Lord James Harrington warmed himself in front of the crackling fire in the dining room at Harrington's, the family manor house that was now a thriving country hotel. He detected a slight smell of apples coming from the logs. It was a late September morning; their guests had finished breakfast and were already busy planning their day. The hotel was now a popular retreat for the wealthy and famous; new activities and interests were being added every year to ensure their guests experienced a relaxing and enjoyable holiday. After studying similar holiday retreats across Europe, particularly along the French Riviera and Italian coasts, James had embraced the best of the ideas he'd seen and incorporated them here to ensure that all needs were catered for.

Today, the guests had dispersed to a number of locations. Some had driven to nearby Brighton for a day at the races; others had journeyed a few miles along the coast to Rottingdean to go horse-riding, while a few had taken advantage of the crisp, autumnal weather to hike along the South Downs. He wandered over to the huge picture windows and gazed at the pale blue sky. The trees in the distance were making their transition from summer green to the rusts and gold of autumn. Their two donkeys, Delphine and Sebastian, munched on apples in the far field and kept the grass at bay.

Beyond him, through the open doors to the reception area, his wife, Beth, and the reverend's wife, Anne Merryweather, were preparing a dazzling display of seasonal flowers. Mrs Jepson, their cleaner both here and at home, was polishing the wooden floor as if her life depended on it. It glistened where the light caught it and he marvelled at how she managed to remove the scuff marks and scrapes that occasionally appeared.

His chef, Didier, obscured his view. His short, rotund form filled the door-frame as he clasped his hands together.

'Lord 'arrington,' he said in a strong French accent. 'My apologies for keeping you waiting.'

James waved the apology aside. He had no desire to criticise his chef unless it was absolutely necessary and that scenario had, fortunately, never reared its head. The man had a chef's temperament and would have no qualms about simply throwing his apron down and resigning if he felt it warranted such action.

He steered his chef toward the nearest table. 'I'm sure what you're about to show me will be worth the wait.'

Didier, impeccably dressed in crisp chef's whites, joined him at the table and spread out two sheets of paper.

'This week, we 'ave the wonderful menu and I, Didier Le Noir, will be foraging the forests.'

'I say, that sounds rather marvellous. What are you foraging for?'

He received an indignant glare. 'Mushrooms, Lord 'arrington.' Didier waved a sheet of paper as he listed them. 'Chanterelles, cèpes, trompettes de la mort, whatever I can find; and I will serve the creamy mushroom soup with your grandmother's bread, *oui?*'

'Ah yes. *Oui, oui,*' said James. 'That sounds rather delicious.'

Grandma Harrington's fresh white bread toasted with cheese would be a perfect accompaniment to Didier's dish.

Didier's chest swelled. 'Such a shame your grandmother is not here, Lord 'arrington — we would, in the kitchen, be a most formidable team.'

James agreed as he perused the rest of the menu. 'You're also doing a French onion soup with the same accompaniment. Splendid.'

'*Mais oui,* and the smoked mackerel pâté for those who pooh-pooh the soup.'

James salivated as he read through the choice of main courses: guinea fowl with porcini mushrooms and bacon; boeuf bourguignon; traditional English steak and kidney pudding. Anticipation rushed through him.

'I say, are you doing my Grandmother's steak and kidney?'

Didier's eyes sparkled. '*Mais oui.* I see from the photograph in the reception that your grandmother was born in late September, so this is in celebration of her passion for excellent food.'

'Then I must book a table. I also see you have a pear tart with chocolate sauce — that'll keep my wife happy.'

His wife's voice floated in from the entrance. 'What'll keep me happy?'

Although she'd lived in England since leaving finishing school, she maintained a slight inflection from her upbringing in Boston.

James called her over to go through the planned menu and suggested they reserve their places. 'Our esteemed chef is also doing an autumn fruit crumble with custard, which sounds rather appetising.'

'It all sounds perfect,' she replied. 'I'm sure our guests will love it. As will I.' She made a point of congratulating Didier on his selection.

Didier's chest swelled further as he rose from his chair. He gathered his papers, proffered a bow and returned to the kitchen.

James congratulated her. 'The way to a chef's heart is to compliment him, darling, and you do it so well.'

'Fiona recommended we do that from the start,' said Beth, recalling the day Didier first arrived.

There was no doubt that the chef was master of his domain. The fact that he was working for a Lord and Lady had not fazed him one jot. Outside the kitchen, he was polite, courteous and a joy to be with. Inside his kitchen empire, he was temperamental and bossy. But the relationship worked well and all three of them knew the boundaries and where not to cross them. In return, James knew he had the best chef in the south-east and paid a good salary to keep him.

James followed Beth through to reception, where Anne was putting the finishing touches to the floral display.

'There, I think that will last for a good week,' she said. 'Put a pinch of sugar in the water in a couple of days. That always gives them a bit of a boost.'

Beth linked arms with her. 'Those rust-coloured chrysanthemums are lovely. And these orange and butternut gerberas are beautiful, don't you think?' She turned to their cleaner. 'What do you think, Mrs Jepson?'

Mrs Jepson brushed a stray hair from her perspiring face before expressing her approval and going back to her polishing. The telephone rang and Paul, the front desk manager and maitre d'hôtel, emerged from the office to answer it. After a brief chat, he held the receiver up.

'It's Detective Chief Inspector Lane, your Lordship.'

DCI George Lane was one of James' oldest friends and, over the last couple of years, he'd helped the Inspector out with a number of mysteries that had cropped up in the area. His participation hadn't always gone down that well with George but his friend had to admit, his insight had resulted in arrests and convictions.

He took the receiver and rested his elbows on the desk. 'Hello, George. Are you confirming our lunchtime snifter? We said one o'clock at the Half Moon.'

'Sorry, James, something's come up. I'll have to cancel.'

'That's a shame. Anything serious?'

'Escaped convict.'

'Oh?'

'Goes by the name of Locksmith Joe.'

James couldn't help but chuckle. 'Sounds like a music hall act. Locksmith Joe was a jolly old soul and a jolly old soul was he.'

He heard George grunt. 'Don't let the name fool you. I'm told he's a cold-blooded killer. We'll be sending a description round to all the stations. He's pretty easy to identify by all accounts. Big bloke, around sixty, with thick grey hair and a bushy beard to match. Been locked up about ten years and I don't think he's one to stop and have a chat with. I'll speak to you later.'

'Right, well, keep us updated and we'll have that drink another time.' He replaced the receiver.

Paul examined the guest book. 'Full house this week, Lord Harrington. I suppose that's the scarecrow festival pulling the crowds in.'

'Yes, it's beginning to get quite a following.'

The scarecrow festival had been a Cavendish tradition for around fifty years.

11

James had no idea how or why it had begun, but he'd assumed that it was simply because of the number of farms in the area and the sheer fun of it.

Every autumn, alongside the traditional harvest festivities, the scarecrow festival had kept growing in popularity. It consisted of a parade along the high street, one circuit around the village green then into a specially erected marquee in front of the Half Moon pub where prizes for the best scarecrow outfit were awarded. The villagers held a number of events on the village green during the year and this was certainly one of the most popular ones on the calendar.

The parade, led by Bob Tanner and his folk band, consisted of villagers and farmers dressed as scarecrows, all vying for the title of Best Cavendish Scarecrow. First prize was a Fortnum and Mason hamper supplied by James and Beth.

James slipped his hands into his pockets. Reception was empty except for Beth, Anne, Paul and Mrs Jepson. 'We apparently have an escaped convict on the loose,' he announced.

Beth and Anne gawped, Mrs Jepson made the sign of the cross, and Paul frowned.

'Is he in this area, your Lordship?'

'I'm assuming so.' He repeated what was said in his conversation with George.

'Should we inform the guests?' Paul continued.

'I don't think there's any need. There's nothing to suggest he's going to come here and we don't want to alarm people unnecessarily.'

A cheery 'Oi, oi,' interrupted them.

James swung round to see another long-standing friend, the flat-capped Bert Briggs, standing in the main doorway. He wore an old tweed jacket and had a newspaper under his arm along with a parcel wrapped in brown paper.

'Bert, what are you doing here?'

He held the parcel out to Beth. 'Wondered where the girls were. I thought you was at the vicarage and Stephen said you was all up 'ere. I borrowed 'is bike cos I didn't wanna cart this lot about.'

Anne's eyes sparkled. 'Is that material?'

'Left over at the markets. Thought it

13

might come in 'andy for something.'

Beth and Anne eagerly accepted the parcel and peeled back the brown paper wrapping. Underneath were a number of plain and patterned fabrics. They excitedly launched into a discussion of various ways of using the material and how it would be ideal for the next Cavendish Players' production. Bert, bemused by how much joy this had brought, left the package with them and wandered across to James. He waved his newspaper.

'I caught the tail end of your chat about Locksmith Joe — made the Brighton paper.' He spread the newspaper on the desk.

James read the article. 'Joe Nesbitt, known as Locksmith Joe, escaped from Wandsworth prison last night and is believed to have journeyed to West Sussex where he is known to have family.' He skimmed the rest of the piece and reeled at the last sentence. 'Locksmith Joe is extremely dangerous and must not be approached under any circumstances.'

Mrs Jepson picked up her bucket and mop and mumbled to herself. 'Won't be safe in our beds. Make sure you lock your doors.'

James assured her she would probably survive the escape of Locksmith Joe. He sought Bert's assurance. 'I mean, it's not as if he has ties in Cavendish, is it?'

Bert gave an unconvincing shrug.

James lowered his voice. 'Do you know him?'

His friend took an unusual interest in his shoes and denied any association. James had known Bert Briggs since a chance meeting during a school outing many moons ago and he knew the chap inside out. At this particular moment, the denial didn't match the body language. He was convinced that Bert almost certainly knew Locksmith Joe but, for some reason, didn't want to share this with him. He tried to probe further but his friend insisted he had to return the bicycle to Stephen. Within a minute, he'd gone.

James watched him disappear down the drive and deliberated. He enjoyed his friendships with both Bert and DCI Lane, but it never ceased to amaze him how the former had not had his collar felt by the latter. He'd worried that, one day, Bert would cross the line and face George Lane officially. Had that day arrived? Did Bert know something about this prison escape? Had Bert had a hand it? He pushed the thought from his mind but, annoyingly, it nudged its way back. Try as he might, he couldn't shift the notion that Bert's behaviour had been most odd.

3

The following morning, James and Beth rapped on the door of a small terraced house close to the junior school. Mr Chrichton, the headmaster of Cavendish Junior, swung the door open with a surprised smile.

'Lord and Lady Harrington.' He beckoned them in. 'I wasn't expecting you.'

James offered a mock salute and stood back to allow Beth to go ahead of him. 'We took a chance that you were in, old chap. You mentioned wanting to discuss the festival and as we were passing we thought we'd stop by.' He jutted his chin out. 'Is now convenient?'

'Of course, of course. Come through.'

They followed his stocky frame to a small, cosy room where he tidied up a number of newspapers and books strewn across the furniture. James couldn't help but smile. Mr Chrichton was an excellent teacher but he displayed the attributes of a typical bachelor. His home, although clean, was nothing short of chaotic.

'Excuse the mess,' he said. 'I'm always telling my pupils to leave things tidy — good job they don't see me at home.'

'Please don't worry on our account,' replied Beth.

After the pleasantries and the distribution of welcome cups of tea, the three of them sat down in wingback armchairs.

James began. 'So, which festival do you want to discuss? Harvest, Scarecrow or Supper?'

'For my part, the Harvest Festival service,' replied Chrichton. 'The children are obviously involved in everything. We want to start rehearsing hymns for the service. I was hoping to see the reverend. You don't happen to know what he's planning or what he wants them to sing, do you?'

James cast a hopeful eye at Beth who was happy to share what she knew. 'I believe that Stephen mentioned he wanted the children to sing 'We Plough the Fields and Scatter'. Everyone knows that and it's *the* traditional harvest hymn. James is going to do a little speech about the farmers.' She shrugged. 'Other than that, I'm afraid I don't have any further details.'

'Our niches are the other two events,' James put in.

'Of course,' said Chrichton. 'I'm really best off hunting the vicar down to establish exactly what his vision is. Will the harvest be in? The weather's been a little on and off this summer.'

'Not sure. But, of course, the Harvest Festival dates are set in stone. Whatever the weather, the supper and service will take place as scheduled.'

'And is the supper taking place at the outbuilding behind the pub?'

'Yes. It's easy for everyone to get to and it's dry. Donovan's just had a new roof put on it so we'll be sheltered from the elements.'

Donovan Delaney, the landlord of the Half Moon, had been keen to get the outbuilding fit for its purpose. That way, any events that could potentially be rained off could be transferred inside if need be.

The Harvest Supper had died out in many regions, but James and Beth had kept the tradition alive and it had become a firm part of their autumn celebrations.

The supper consisted of a huge feast of goose stuffed with apples and vegetables, originally laid on by the farming community but now with the whole village contributing something. This year, a few joints of gammon cooked in cider were being added to the menu.

At every supper, a caraway seed cake was prepared to distribute to everyone. This had originally been served to the farm workers to keep their strength up and, again, James had kept the tradition going. This year, it was the turn of Rose and Lilac Crumb, the 'Snoop Sisters' to bake the cake. He'd nicknamed them the Snoop Sisters after they moved to the village several years ago. Their busybody ways infuriated many. But, much as he loathed their interfering, he'd learnt just a few months ago that, if they felt they were the centre of attention, they tended to integrate better.

Chrichton sat back and sipped his tea. 'Excuse me for changing the subject, but have you met the people up at Cory House?'

'I've swung by on a couple of occasions, but I've not received any answer.

Beth hasn't had a chance to visit yet.'

'No, I must get around to doing that. Stephen must have met them, darling. You know how he loves to make everyone feel part of the community.'

'He's tried on numerous occasions,' said James. 'Anne, too. He's now resorted to a rather underhand method.'

Beth tilted her head. 'Underhand?'

'Stephen's seen the curtains twitch but they don't answer the door. So, our reverend is going to wait until he sees the lady of the house return from her shopping or whatever she does and pounce.'

Chrichton chuckled. 'And when is he proposing to do that?'

James checked his watch. 'In around thirty minutes. The lady of the house has taken to shopping in Haywards Heath on a Wednesday morning. Stephen's worked out her timetable. I said I'd meet him there.'

Beth laughed. 'So you're in on this, too?' She gave an eager look. 'Well, if you're going, you'd best take me as well.'

He grinned and promised that he had no intention of leaving her behind.

Chrichton scratched his head. 'They've been here a few weeks now and I don't even know who they are. Do you?'

'Actually, yes,' replied James. 'Christie and Jeannie Cameron — moved from Yorkshire.'

Beth stared. 'How on earth did you know that?'

James explained that the postman had delivered mail there. The same postman had also seen mail forwarded on to Cory House that had been originally addressed to the village of Otley, near Bradford.

'It's odd that they've not shown themselves.'

Chrichton sat forward. 'Not as odd as the stories the local children have started.'

James and Beth instinctively edged closer as Chrichton continued.

'They're positive they've seen a ghost at an upstairs window.'

Beth pulled a disbelieving face and James almost choked on his tea. 'A ghost?'

Chrichton grimaced and shrugged. 'They're certain they've seen it. Even the reverend's kiddies. I know children have an imagination, but some of them seemed quite resolute about it — a face at the window — a young man.' He placed his drink on a side table and picked up an old book. 'It's an old house; parts of it date back to the seventeenth century. This book mentions a ghost at Cory House but it doesn't go into much detail.'

'Who *was* Cory?' said Beth.

James straightened a seam in his trousers. 'Cory was the name of the family who lived there. The name died out around 1890 I believe, when a fire destroyed part of the roof and finished the last Cory off with it. It's been empty for around twenty years now. Not sure who owned it. Last people there rented it. Surprised anyone's taken it on — it must be in need of some repair.'

Chrichton agreed. 'I understand the structure is actually quite sound. It was built by professional masons, so it'll be standing long after you and I have moved on; but it would be incredibly damp. The gardens are overgrown and I notice that ivy has taken hold on the front-facing wall.'

Beth winced. 'That can transform a

house, but it doesn't do anything for the structure.' She turned to James. 'Do you remember your sister having that ivy removed from her house? They had to restore the walls once they'd finished.' Her eyes lit up. 'But if the last Cory died in the house, that may be the ghost. The fire destroyed the roof and the children *have* seen a figure upstairs.'

James chuckled. 'You're as bad as the children. There's probably a perfectly reasonable explanation. Perhaps they have someone staying with them — a relative or a friend.' He pushed himself up, thanked Chrichton for his hospitality and helped Beth to her feet. 'Well, darling, it's been a while since we've had anything to investigate. Let's meet Stephen and see what we can find out about the Camerons.'

She held his hand. 'And, more importantly, their ghost.'

4

James slipped down through the gears and steered the Austin Healey through the entrance to Cory House.

'Goodness,' Beth whispered. 'I don't know about Cory House, I'd liken this more to Bleak House.'

'You're not wrong there. It is in need of significant care and attention.'

He remembered having seen pictures of the residence back in its glory days. A large, square house with, he recalled, four rooms upstairs and four downstairs, including the kitchen. It was a secluded building; more so now the surrounding trees and shrubs had grown unattended for decades. A landscape gardener could whip this into shape and it would make all the difference. He manoeuvred the car around established weeds. A builder's van was parked outside and its owner was on a ladder clearing away the ivy on the front wall.

'Looks like they're making a start on some renovation.'

Ahead of them was the angular figure of the Reverend Stephen Merryweather who was positioning his bicycle against the wall. He was dressed formally in a black suit and polished shoes. His hand reached up to ensure his dog collar was secure before he waved a greeting.

James grabbed a bottle of sherry from the back seat and ran round to open the door for Beth. He called across to Stephen. 'Did you think we weren't coming?'

'F-for a while, yes,' he said with his endearing stammer. 'This is a frustrating exercise on my own. P-perhaps we'll have more success en masse.'

Approaching the vicar, James lowered his voice. 'You obviously didn't catch her.'

Stephen made a frustrated expression and said he hadn't been quick enough to catch up with the lady of the house. 'I'm pretty s-sure she sensed I was on her tail. She was carrying t-two bags of shopping and moved at an alarming speed.'

'Then let us waste no more time,' said

James as he mounted the steps. He pushed the doorbell and, for good measure, hammered twice on the door. Beth glared at him. He shrugged. 'They may be hard of hearing.'

They stood for two minutes, glancing at the door, peering through the side window, wondering when to repeat the process. James pressed the bell again and hammered on the door even harder than before.

'James!' Beth said.

He retreated with feigned innocence. Beth drew her wool scarf around her neck and, instinctively, James did the same. The weather cast a chill, but this place felt several degrees cooler. Stephen checked his watch. He was about to speak when a gruff voice shouted from the other side of the front door.

'What do ye want?'

Stephen appeared startled by the abrupt tone. James took the lead.

'Ah, Mr Cameron?'

'What's it to you?'

James wasn't expecting such an aggressive greeting. He stuck his chin out. 'We are Lord and Lady Harrington and the Reverend Stephen Merryweather. We've been trying to get hold of you as we'd like to formally welcome you and your wife to the village.'

He put his ear to the door and caught the helpless expressions on Beth and Stephen's faces.

'Mr Cameron, we won't keep you,' shouted James. 'We know you're probably busy and all, but we're keen to meet you and hope that — '

The key in the lock turned. James waited for the door to open but it remained closed. Beth pulled his sleeve and whispered, 'You don't think he locked it, do you?'

James was about to speak when he saw the huge bronze doorknob turn and the panelled oak door edged open. Cameron's ruddy face peered out.

'We're not ones for socialising.'

James smiled and held up the bottle of sherry. 'And we're not for forcing you to, Mr Cameron. We are a close-knit community and, if you prefer no intrusion, we will not intrude. However, for the sake of one neighbourly visit, will you allow us a few minutes?'

Cameron scrutinised the three of them until, finally, he held the door open and snatched the bottle of sherry. 'You'll not stop pestering me until I do. First room on the left.'

They gave each other sideways looks and entered the hallway. In front of them was another workman toward the back of the house in what James thought was a downstairs cloakroom. They wandered through to a large, square living room with a high ceiling, where a small log fire burned.

Beth headed straight to it and held her palms up to feel the warmth. 'I would imagine you need a few of these to warm the house through,' she said. 'It had been empty for quite some time, you know.'

Cameron, dressed in wool trousers and an oversized Aran sweater, appeared nonplussed. 'We've fires in the rooms we use — no more.' He went to the door and called out. 'Jeannie, we've visitors.' He reluctantly waved at the various seating options in the room.

James chose one of the armchairs by the window. He was pleased that Cameron hadn't asked for his jacket and scarf. But, having thought about it, it seemed unlikely that the man would encourage any lengthy stay. Although the fire was welcome, the room emanated damp and felt unusually cold. Beth sat on a fireside chair and shuddered. Stephen stood alongside. He threw James a concerned frown. James returned it with a raised eyebrow. The atmosphere was unwelcoming to say the least.

Footsteps coming along the hall directed James' gaze to the door, where Jeannie appeared. He stood up. She wiped her hands on a towel and focussed on Stephen.

'You're persistent, I'll give ye that.'

'F-forgive me, Mrs Cameron, I — '

'It's *Miss* Cameron.' She drew herself up. 'You're here now, so you'd best sit down. Tea, brother?'

Cameron nodded and took his seat by the fire. His sister turned back down the passageway.

'I'm sorry, Mr Cameron,' said James. 'We thought you were husband and wife.'

Cameron gazed into the fire. 'She's taken her place with the Lord. Jeannie moved in — she never married.'

In the uncomfortable silence that followed, they waited for tea. The three of them attempted to converse with Cameron, but they received little more than a yes or no. Beth, usually beguiling with her winning smile and inquisitive nature, also failed to break the ice. Jeannie reappeared with a tea tray. The stillness was filled with the crackling fire, the ticking mantel clock and chinking of crockery. Stephen cleared his throat and began the story of his own welcome to the village just under a year previously.

'E-everyone was so friendly and Lord and Lady Harrington keep many traditional events and f-festivals running. It creates a w-wonderful community spirit.'

'That's one of the reasons we're here, actually,' said James. 'We have a number of activities over the next couple of weeks, what with harvest time coming, so we thought you might want to join us. We have the scarecrow festival in the next couple of days, then the Harvest Festival.

After that, we have a harvest supper in the stone barn behind the Half Moon.'

'Scarecrow festival?' Cameron's eyes narrowed. 'We'll not join you for any pagan rites.'

James saw Beth bristle.

'I say, it's nothing untoward,' said James. 'Just a bit of fun where the locals try and outdo one another in the costume stakes. I don't believe scarecrows go back to pagan times, Mr Cameron.'

Stephen gave him a covert shake of the head and directed his eyes to the wall above the fireplace. James followed his gaze and saw a simple wooden cross. He then noticed the bible stand and the bulky family bible open upon it. On the wall to the side was a dusty old tapestry with the words 'We Live by Faith' embroidered on it. As his eyes scanned the sparse room, he realised that, the little decoration there was, highlighted a strict religious belief and nothing else.

He shifted awkwardly. 'Well, perhaps not the scarecrow festival, but you'll join us at church for the Harvest Festival service, surely?'

The silence in the room left James feeling uneasy. A sound above distracted him. Creaking floorboards? Footsteps? Cameron, oblivious to any noise, thrust an arthritic finger at Stephen.

'You're one of these modern types, aye?'

'M-modern?'

'You'll no' be preaching against scarecrow festivals?'

'A-absolutely not, Mr C-Cameron. As Lord Harrington specified, it's simply a parade — no religious connotation.' Stephen cast an anxious look at James.

'I say, Stephen here will conduct an excellent harvest service,' said James. 'We'll certainly not pester you to join events that aren't to your taste.' He made a cursory gesture toward the decor. 'You're obviously a man of faith and — '

Cameron slammed the arm of his chair with a fist. 'Aye, I am and I don't need the likes of you and your modern ways.'

Beth leapt up to help Jeannie fill her cup. 'Let me help you with that.' She added milk and forced a nervous smile. 'What part of Scotland are you from?'

'Glasgow.'

Cameron scowled.

'Really? We've not been to that particular area, have we James? James has family near Inverness. This must be quite a change from Glasgow.'

'We've no need for city ways,' Jeannie said.

'But our postman indicated that you'd moved from Yorkshire. What made you move all the way down here?'

Jeannie ignored the question. Beth sat back down with a helpless shrug to James, who loosened his collar and surveyed the room. A shiver went through him at the faint creaking of floorboards. His attention was drawn to the ceiling; a sense of trepidation churned in his stomach. Perhaps the children were right — perhaps the place was haunted. Sitting here in the daytime was giving him the heebie-jeebies. What on earth was it like in the dead of night?

He silently admonished himself for thinking such foolish thoughts and decided the occupants of the house were responsible for this atmosphere. They were decidedly hostile. His gaze darted from the ceiling to the Camerons and out to the hall. Was someone else in the house? Perhaps there was another workman upstairs. The floorboards above creaked again.

Cameron leant forward to stoke the fire. 'Jeannie, we've need for more logs.'

Stephen offered to help collect some wood, but James insisted he remain chatting with the Camerons. 'I'll grab some firewood for you, Miss Cameron. I wonder if I could use your lavatory?' On seeing a workman walk past the doorway he added: 'I'm presuming you have another upstairs?'

Jeannie scrutinised him for longer than was necessary. She jerked her head to the hallway. 'Logs are on the side unit — two logs will suit.' She signalled to the stairs. 'Upstairs, on your right.'

Jeannie's eyes were still on him as he collected two logs and handed them to her. He smiled politely and trotted up the stairs to the lavatory. He glimpsed back and was relieved to see her remain with the others in the lounge.

He held the door ajar and listened. He could hear Beth talking about Cavendish and the various residents. He peered down the landing and saw three further rooms, all with their doors closed. The floorboards creaked from the room above the lounge — the one facing him now. It wouldn't hurt to take a peek in. He slipped out and tiptoed across the landing and turned the doorknob.

'Damn,' he mumbled.

Squatting down, James squinted through the keyhole. He caught his breath as a shadow passed. It was so fast he wondered if he'd imagined it. The room was dimmed and the curtains closed, but James was sure he could see a candle flicker. Downstairs, Beth started coughing with unnatural force. He slipped back to the lavatory, flushed the cistern, and returned to the lounge where he was greeted with suspicious looks by both Jeannie and Christie. He clapped his hands together.

'Well, we promised not to outstay our welcome, so I believe we should make tracks.'

Beth and Stephen rose from their chairs and reiterated their welcome to the Camerons.

'I-I may not be your cup of tea, faith-wise, but the d-doors of our church will always be open to you,' said Stephen.

Cameron grunted. Jeannie focussed on her slippers.

'And,' added Beth, 'the Women's Institute is thriving in Cavendish. So, Miss Cameron, I do hope you'll join us for an evening.'

Christie Cameron remained sitting. Jeannie fidgeted with her hanky as she herded them into the hall and opened the front door.

James mustered a strained smile. 'I'll pop back with a leaflet about the harvest festivities. You may change your mind and want to join us.'

He received a fake smile.

'We'll see.'

The front door closed on them. They stared at one another, unsure of what to say or how to describe their encounter.

James eventually nudged the others onto the drive and slipped his gloves on. 'I don't think I've ever met a frostier couple.'

'Me neither,' said Beth. 'They were as cold as that house. D'you know, we didn't find out one little thing about them, except that they're originally from Glasgow and moved from Yorkshire.'

'And we found that out from the postman.'

'I-I doubt we'll see them at a-any functions,' said Stephen.

James agreed. 'You know the old cliche, you can lead a horse to water but you can't make it drink.' He suggested they put the visit behind them. They did have some residents who didn't involve themselves as much as others and it was neither here nor there to James. For some reason though, this couple had got under his skin and he felt a sense of anger at their comments on the forthcoming events.

'Let's get back. We're meeting later at the Half Moon to discuss everything. The scarecrow festival is this weekend and we need to start making arrangements for the harvest supper.'

'I-I'm sure Anne is free,' replied Stephen. 'The children and Radley are staying with their grandparents overnight.' Radley was a springer spaniel they'd rescued during the summer. Stephen took off his dog collar, undid the top button on his shirt and climbed on his bicycle. 'I'll see you at the pub.'

He pushed himself off and pedalled down the drive. James and Beth got into the car; she turned to him.

'What did you do upstairs?'

'Mmm?'

She playfully punched him. 'You didn't need the lavatory, you fraud. What were you up to? Searching for ghosts? And how did you know the lavatory was upstairs?'

The curtains in the house twitched. He selected first gear and steered the car down the drive.

'Lucky guess. I saw the workman doing repairs in the downstairs lavatory and hoped they may have another. I don't know anything about ghosts, but did you get the feeling there was someone else in the house?'

Beth sat back and pondered. 'I did have a strange feeling in there, but I couldn't place it. I think it may simply be the welcome we received, or the lack of a welcome. Their evasiveness made me uneasy.'

'Well, I heard shuffling above me and boards creaking as if someone was tip-toeing across the floor so, while you were trying your damndest to communicate with those people, I went to take a peek inside the room above where we were sitting.'

'And?'

'Locked.'

'That's strange.'

'But there was definitely someone in there.'

He described the ghostly figure and the flickering candle.

'But why would they have someone in a locked room?'

'Why indeed?'

5

That lunchtime, James parked their other car, a gleaming red Jaguar saloon, on the road by the village green where Donovan Delaney, landlord of the Half Moon pub, heaved on one of many ropes attached to a huge marquee. He was joined by several villagers, their shirtsleeves rolled up, heaving the tent upright while, under the canopy, a large contingent were pushing thick, wooden poles into place. Giving directions through a megaphone was Charlie Hawkins, the amiable librarian.

'Nearly there!' he shouted. 'One more haul on the count of three and that should do it. Ready? One ... two ... three!'

James and Beth climbed out of the car to hear a mass groan as the final effort to secure the tent succeeded. Those who had simply observed the assembly scurried to their allotted positions to drive pegs into the ground and make safe the structure, inside and out. After much huffing and puffing, the work was complete and people gave each other congratulatory pats on the back. Kate, Donovan's petite wife, stood in the doorway of the pub, loudly rapping a tin tray with a wooden spoon.

'King and Barnes barrel is ready,' she announced.

James steered Beth toward the pub. 'I believe they have the new Autumn Gold on tap. Shall we try it?'

Inside, the age-old smell of hops and tobacco smoke greeted them. Stephen and Anne waved them across to the booth overlooking the green. Sitting with them was the butcher, Graham Porter, and Dorothy Forbes, self-appointed director of the Cavendish Players.

Above the din of chatter, James put in an order for a pint and half of Autumn Gold and indicated where they would be sitting. Donovan nodded and reached up for some glasses. At the booth, James and Beth took their places alongside their friends. A few seconds later, their drinks arrived and James held his glass up.

'To the Autumn Gold. Cheers, every-one.'

They raised their glasses and it wasn't long before talk turned to the scarecrow festival.

'Is it all starting at the normal time?' asked Graham.

Dorothy scrutinised the timetable attached to her ever-present clipboard. A stalwart of the Cavendish Players, she was the definition of efficiency and, although she could be somewhat annoying in her demands, James was pleased to see someone take charge and instil a sense of fear in anyone crossing her. One look from Dorothy and you did as you were told. She was certainly someone he turned to when these events came around.

'The scarecrows will start the parade into the village at ten o'clock in the morning,' she began. 'It'll take the normal route along the high street by the school playground. The scarecrows will follow Bob Tanner and his band down the high street and around the village green. Judging takes place at eleven o'clock in the marquee.' Dorothy peered over her glasses;

her gaze settled on Graham. 'Mr Porter, you are supplying the normal hog roast?'

Graham's ruddy face grinned. 'Of course. Nice bit of pork this year. They've been munching on Pete Mitchell's apples for the last month so should be a nice succulent bit of meat. We'll have apple sauce and crackling as well, to put in the rolls.'

Pete Mitchell owned the orchard two miles up the road from James and Beth and regularly supplied greengrocers and cider companies with his apples and pears. Any that were too bruised or soft went to Graham's swine.

Dorothy checked her notes. 'Most satisfactory. The WI has three tables and Mr and Mrs Delaney are setting up a bar in the marquee.' She reached across and tapped the table hard. Stephen sat up with a start. 'Reverend Merryweather, are you doing anything?'

He sat up. 'I-I didn't think I was. My preparations are for the Harvest Festival. I could say a prayer if you th-think it appropriate.'

A murmur went round the table, the general consensus being that this wasn't a good idea. Anne gently elbowed him. 'I think the Harvest Festival and supper are more your thing, darling.'

'Lord Harrington,' asked Dorothy, 'I trust you're giving out the prizes as normal?'

'I'm down to do so, but I wondered if Professor Wilkins might want to stand in?' James went on to explain that Wilkins was knowledgeable on the history of scarecrows and it would make a change for the Professor to be more involved. 'What d'you think?'

There was another murmur of support: James made a mental note to put the idea to Wilkins. Dorothy examined her clipboard.

'The judging of vegetables will be straight after the distribution of prizes to the scarecrows. Mr Bennett is down to judge the vegetables.'

'Splendid,' said James. His boyhood fishing tutor was a true countryman and would relish the role. What he didn't know about growing vegetables could be written on the back of a postage stamp.

'The WI is also holding a chutney

competition,' continued Dorothy.

Beth sipped her drink. 'Is our mad solicitor doing any singing?'

'Of course. Mr Bateson is writing something especially for the scarecrow festival. The Cubs and Brownies are going to sing 'Oats and Beans and Barley' as the scarecrows enter the marquee.'

'All sounds rather jolly, doesn't it?' said James with a smile.

Graham leant forward. 'And are we being graced with the presence of our new residents?'

'I've yet to meet them,' said Anne. 'Three times I've knocked on their door and I know they're in. They're terribly stand-offish.'

'The C-Camerons will be giving the scarecrow parade a miss,' said Stephen. 'They are strict Presbyterian, almost Victorian in their values, and feel this is unnecessary frivolity during harvest t-time.'

'Poppycock,' said Graham. 'Harvest is a celebration. We're a community; it's a bit of fun to bring the village together.' He poked a finger at Stephen. 'You've met 'im?'

Stephen smiled and studied his fingers. 'Yes. I-I must be welcoming to all, I know, but I did find the Camerons a little d-difficult to engage with.'

The same question was directed at James, who grimaced. 'Ditto the reverend. The pair of them are exceptionally old school in respect of their faith and may not even attend the Harvest Festival service. Our Stephen could be too modern for their ways.'

Dorothy's glare was most judgemental. 'I do hope they won't spoil the spirit of community we have in Cavendish.'

'He's already had run-ins with a few of us,' said Graham.

'Really?' said James. 'He's only been here a few weeks. Who's he upset?'

Graham held his empty glass in the air and requested another pint before proceeding to elaborate on his statement. Christie Cameron, it appeared, was less than gracious in any dealings or chance meetings in the village. His sister, Jeannie, had annoyed all the shopkeepers by refusing to purchase goods locally, preferring instead to visit the Mac Fisheries in nearby Haywards Heath. Mac Fisheries was the new multi-trading shop that sold meat, fish, dairy and tinned products all in the one store.

Graham continued. 'He's just plain bloody rude, excuse my language, and her boycotting our parade of shops is not on. She lives in Cavendish, she should shop in Cavendish. We've got everything here, so why go all the way to Haywards Heath?'

James squeezed Beth's hand. 'What do you think, darling?'

'Well, I don't think they'll spoil the community just because they decide not to join in. My impression is they'll keep themselves to themselves. We won't even be aware they live here.' She smiled at Stephen. 'Much as we love your services, they may find a church somewhere else that meets their approval. They certainly have their odd little ways and I guess we'll have to respect that.'

Everyone groaned but agreed that they'd best leave the Camerons alone, although Dorothy did enquire why on earth they moved in the first place.

'They moved from Yorkshire,' she said. 'Is that true, your Lordship?'

James confirmed that it was true; that they were originally from Scotland and he'd no idea why they moved so far south.

Anne's eyes danced. 'And you heard the ghost, didn't you?'

All eyes were upon James, who grinned and opted for discretion. 'I did hear something, yes. But it's an old house so it was probably creaking floorboards or something.'

Graham insisted it wasn't and went on to highlight how terrified his children had been when they came home from school the previous week. James listened as the butcher described the events.

'They come home that way sometimes. If it's a nice day, they'll cross the fields and come round the side of Cory House before coming back into the village. The fence is caved in at the back so they scamper about. You know what kids are like. My lot play in the river and mess about before tea-time pretending to own the property. Well, they swear they saw a ghost in the upstairs window. Pale and drawn he was with long spindly fingers and hollow eyes. Little Georgina was in a right state when she got home.' He lowered his voice. 'And Charlie Hawkins' kids have seen it, too.'

Anne couldn't contain herself. 'There, I told you.' She nudged Stephen. 'Mark and Luke have also seen it and they've been rummaging around that pile of rubbish in the back yard along with the rest of the children.'

Try as he might, James couldn't quell the rumours of ghostly spectres and he asserted that in his eyes ghosts did not exist. Silently, though, he did believe a third person resided at Cory House. Ghost or no ghost, he'd seen something, or someone, cross that room; just thinking about it brought back that sense of unease. Perhaps by visiting again the next day, this time with the festival flyers, he could quell that anxiety and get to the bottom of things.

6

The following morning, Beth replaced the telephone receiver on its cradle and positively beamed at James.

'That was Anne. GJ has proposed to Catherine.' She gently clapped her hands and skipped across to embrace him. 'Isn't that wonderful news? We told you they were a perfect match.'

James grinned and pulled her close. Goodness, what a year this had been. It was during the spring they'd found GJ sleeping rough in the old stables at Harrington's, suffering with amnesia. After much adventure and intrigue, he and Beth had discovered his identity, traced his family and provided him with an income. GJ was their nickname for him; a shortened version of Gentleman Jim — the name thrust on him by staff at the East End Mission who had taken him in off the streets of London. At the time, he had no memory of his name but, well-spoken, with impeccable manners and a charming smile that melted the ladies' hearts, the nickname suited him and had stuck. And, once aware of his family ties, the young man decided he preferred GJ over his real name, Sebastian.

During the investigation into GJ, it had become apparent that he was an artist of exceptional ability and James offered him the use of the old stables to set up an artist studio, workshop and gallery. He'd held his first workshop during the summer and the delightful Catherine was one of his first pupils. Beth pushed away and wagged a finger.

'We're under strict instructions not to say anything. Only we, Bert and the Merryweathers know. I think GJ wants to get in touch with his aunt and adoptive parents before announcing it.'

'That's wonderful,' said James. 'Which means we'll be seeing the delightful aunt again.'

James and Beth had a soft spot for Miss Brooks-Hunter, an elderly yet spritely spinster, who had so impressed them with her stories of wartime bravery alongside her sister, Delphine.

'And the not so delightful Mrs Crabtree,' added Beth.

'Yes, although I must admit I believe she has warmed a little since our first meeting.'

James slipped his sheepskin jacket on and picked up a handful of festival flyers. He waved them at Beth. 'I'm popping these over to the Camerons; one last attempt to get them to integrate and all that.'

He noticed Beth's sagging posture and kissed her forehead. 'At least we can say we've tried.'

'That's if you can get them to answer the door,' replied Beth. 'Bet you sixpence you come back with those flyers.'

He winked at her. 'Not if I post them through the letterbox.'

He did wonder if the front door would remain closed when he knocked but, as he pulled into the drive, he found himself lost for words. Two police cars were parked outside the house and a young constable stood guard at the entrance.

James drew up to one side, grabbed the leaflets and examined the vehicles as he walked toward the house.

'I say, Constable, what's going on?'

James had recognised PC Black, the policeman from their escapades during the summer. The young man saluted.

'Hello, your Lordship. Seems like the man of the house is dead, sir.'

James stopped in his tracks. 'What? Mr Cameron? When?'

'During the night we think, sir. I mean, Miss Cameron said he was fine last night. Suspicious, we think — well, the guv'nor doesn't, the doc does.'

'George inside?'

The constable stiffened. 'No sir, DCI Lane had something on. He's coming along shortly. His colleague is helping out for this morning. He's upstairs with a photographer.'

James held a hand up. 'Say no more. Does Miss Cameron need some company?'

The constable gave him a helpless shrug. Before James could answer, the front door opened and a thin, skeletal figure of a man appeared, in a suit that might have fitted once but now hung loosely. He had a swarthy complexion and James couldn't help but liken him to a used car salesman.

'Who's this?' the skeleton said.

The constable pulled his shoulders back. 'Lord Harrington, sir.'

'What's he doing here?'

The young man straightened up and his face paled. James held out a welcoming hand. The man, a rather oily-looking individual, made no move toward him. James waved the leaflets.

'I popped by to deliver these about the Harvest Festivals.'

The skeleton tilted his head. 'Lord Harrington? You're the bloke that thinks he's a bit of sleuth.'

James chuckled. 'And you are?'

'Inspector Collins.'

James repeated his question about whether Miss Cameron required company during this time. Collins reacted as if he hadn't thought of such a thing. But then he apparently decided it wouldn't be any skin off his nose if James wanted to dish out some soothing words. Upon entering Cory House, James heard the inspector mumble.

'You might get more sense out of her than me.'

Inside the living room where he'd been seated the previous day, he was greeted by Dr Philip Jackson. If anyone was capable of soothing a distressed woman, James felt it would be Philip. His calm and relaxed character would no doubt quieten his patient down. But then, he remembered, this was Jeannie Cameron, a woman who didn't seem to have any warmth about her whatsoever.

'And where is the lady of the house?'

'She's just popped to the kitchen,' Philip said as he wandered over to him. 'Have you met her?'

'Yesterday, for the first time.'

'What d'you make of her?'

James said that, from what little he'd observed, she was a bitter humourless spinster who might have been dealt a better hand had circumstances dictated. 'Sorry, that's a rather rotten thing to say. I don't know her circumstances and she's lost her brother. I should really be saying that I feel the family has perhaps been dealt a bad hand,' he added.

'I agree with everything you've said,' said Philip. 'I only asked because I wondered if she was all there, that's all.'

James tilted his head with an inquisitive air.

Philip stepped toward him. 'Well, she started hissing at me, telling me to mind my own business. Then she said her brother was murdered, then — '

'Murdered? Who by for goodness' sake?'

Philip shrugged as James lowered his voice further.

'You're the doctor, what do you think?'

'I'll have to leave it to the police to make that call. He took what appears to be an overdose of sleeping draught, but there is slight bruising around the neck. Not prominent, but it needs investigating for sure. I'm not signing anything off. I'll leave it to the coroner.' He frowned.

James waited.

'Thing is, he's only been dead a few hours and the door was locked from the inside. I'm not sure how anyone could have got in to kill him.'

'Was the key still in the lock?'

'Yes,' replied Philip, 'so I can't see how it was murder.' He looked at James. 'And she's the only other person living here, so she's setting herself up to be prime suspect.'

Footsteps in the hall interrupted their thoughts.

'The ambulance is here to take the body away,' said Inspector Collins. 'Do you need to see anything else, Doctor?'

Philip snapped his bag shut. 'I don't think so, Inspector. I'll type up my notes and get them over to you this afternoon. Can the coroner not get here? Bearing in mind the sister's accusation?'

Collins ignored Jackson. 'Appreciate your time, Doctor. You can get along to your own patients now.' The inspector trudged up the stairs and was quickly followed by Jeannie, who insisted on saying prayers before her brother's body was taken.

James turned to Philip. 'Have you given her a sedative or anything?'

Philip replied with a helpless shrug. 'Said she didn't need one. Perhaps it's delayed shock or she's so practical that she gets on with it. Strangely enough, I think it's the latter.'

He patted James on the arm and bade him goodbye. James followed him out to the hall and watched as the medical team stretchered Cameron's body down the stairs and into the waiting ambulance. Collins turned to Jeannie Cameron, reiterated his condolences and announced that he'd be in touch. He said a curt goodbye to James and left.

An uncomfortable silence followed and James struggled to make eye contact with Jeannie. Her very presence made him uncomfortable.

He gave himself a mental dressing down for being so selfish. 'I'm so sorry to learn about your brother, Miss Cameron. I know I only met him the once, but you must be distraught, especially as you're new to the area. I want you — '

'I've no need for company.'

'Right.' He folded the leaflets and slipped them into his pocket.

She scowled at him. 'That Inspector, Collins, he accused you of prying.'

James flinched. 'I beg your pardon?'

'Prying.'

'I believe he did nothing of the sort, Miss Cameron.' James put his gloves on and made to leave.

She crossed her arms and almost stepped in front of him. 'It's what I call amateur sleuths. Busybodies, prying into affairs they've no business with.'

James forced himself to smile. 'With every respect, Miss Cameron, you don't know me or how I have assisted the police. Again, let me offer you my sincere condolences. However, as I was going to say before you interrupted me, if you'd like me to ask the Reverend Merry-weather to call, I can certainly do so.'

She turned away, replying in an abrasive tone. 'You'll want to see the room. Aye, the Inspector had no interest in what I'd to say. Perhaps you will.' She mounted the stairs.

James frowned and wondered whether to leave her to her ramblings and go; but his own curiosity got the better of him and he opted to follow her. They passed the locked room above the living room to the bedroom next door. He studied the floor with concern. Splinters of wood were strewn on the floor and the lock on the door hung at an awkward angle.

He squatted down to examine it. 'You had to force the door?'

'Aye.'

James noted the locked room next door. 'We?'

'I'd difficulty getting in with brother's morning tea. I knocked, but he . . . ' Jeannie smoothed her apron down. 'He wouldn't waken, so I summoned the postman. He'd arrived with a delivery. He broke the lock and there he was.'

James scanned the room. On the table by the bed was a ring mark from what was, presumably, the previous night's milky drink. The room was as bare as the front room downstairs. There was a small dressing table underneath the window, a wardrobe, a tiny sink and a patterned rug covering uneven floorboards.

'Does . . . did he always lock his bedroom door?'

Jeannie clasped her hands together. 'Aye.'

'Can I ask why?'

She averted her eyes. James was about to probe for more information, when a noise distracted him below. Downstairs in the hall, he saw his good friend, DCI Lane, gazing up, his trilby rolling in his hand.

'Ah, George, your colleague left a few minutes ago.'

George said that he'd passed him on the road, but felt he should call in and ensure that everything was in order. James, followed by Jeannie Cameron, descended the stairs, where George introduced himself.

'My condolences to you, Miss Cameron. I shan't trespass on your time. I trust Inspector Collins didn't cause too much distress? It's difficult, I know, when someone dies unexpectedly.'

'Is that what you think, Mr Lane?'

George shifted his gaze at James and then to Miss Cameron. 'Don't you?'

Jeannie Cameron peeked over her shoulder to the stairs, opened her mouth to speak and then closed it again. Her hands checked her hair, which was pinned back so tight that it stretched her forehead.

'If you've nothing further, I've a funeral to arrange,' she said.

George held his ground. 'Miss Cameron, is there something you wish to tell me? Do you suspect this to be something other than a normal death?'

She brought her chin in and folded her arms. 'He was a man of faith; a strict God-fearing man who would never sin against the Father.' Her eyes went to the ceiling. 'He'll have done it.'

James frowned.

'God?' said George.

Her posture was stiff. 'You'll not mock the Lord, Mr Lane.'

George assured her he was doing nothing of the sort. 'But I thought it was just you and your brother living here.'

'Aye, that's right.' She smoothed her apron down and chivvied them toward the front door. 'I've arrangements to make. You'll be leaving now.'

James opened the front door and, after

receiving a curt goodbye, ushered George out and down the steps to the gravel drive. The door slammed behind them.

'Good grief,' said George. 'She's an odd one.'

James agreed and examined the old house. 'You've heard about the local children seeing ghosts here, have you?'

His friend chuckled. 'If you're short of something to do, James, you can always get on with your festivals.'

With a wry smile, James gave an account of his visit the previous day. He told George about the feeling that someone else was in the house; the locked room above the lounge and the fleeting shape seen through the keyhole.

'Did you speak with your Inspector chap? Did he tell you what Jackson said?'

Seeing George's puzzlement, James then described the slight bruising. His friend bristled and cursed Collins for not letting him know. James continued.

'Philip's leaving this one to your people.' He tightened his lips. 'There's someone else in that house, George. It's not a ghost. The room was dimly lit and shadows with arms and legs tend to mean a living, breathing being.'

George's eyes darted from James to the house and back again. He heaved a frustrated sigh and trudged back up the steps to knock politely on the door. Jeannie Cameron screeched from the back of the house.

'Will ye no' leave us in peace? An eye for an eye. He'll pay for what he's done; God will send his justice.'

James pulled a face at George, who hammered firmly on the door. 'Miss Cameron, open up please.'

'God will punish those who punish others,' she said as she opened the door. A wisp of hair had fallen over her forehead. 'You'll not take him. God will deal with him.'

James gently steered her into the hall and looked up to the ceiling. 'Miss Cameron, who are you shielding up there? The room that's locked, who's in there?'

She spat her reply. 'An evil cast upon us.'

7

George placed his trilby on the hall table and instructed Miss Cameron to take them upstairs. Her eyes were like spikes but he simply returned her gaze with a stern expression. James observed the confrontation and that, although Jeannie Cameron was a formidable woman, George's steely eye could make the strongest of people wilt. She sneered, delved in her apron pocket for a set of keys and marched up the stairs. He and George followed. On the landing, she picked out a large key and inserted it in the lock. James' heart quickened — his mouth dry as she flung the door open.

He peered in.

It was a double aspect room and the curtains were drawn across both windows. Opposite, on an old table, sat a half-made model Spitfire, scattered pieces of the structure, plus a detailed diagram of how to build it, along with a small tube of glue. Three desk lamps lit what appeared to be a large room with a small coal fire. Behind the desk were shelves housing finished model aircraft that had been painted exquisitely. In the subdued lighting, he saw a small bed and, at the other side of the room, an armchair and a sofa. In the corner stood a record player.

From the gloom, a movement caught his eye. He nudged George and pointed and, as his friend reacted, a figure stepped further back. James kept his eyes firmly on the vague shape while he addressed Miss Cameron.

'Miss Cameron, who is this?'

Although she stood behind him, James could imagine her eyes narrowing. He could almost feel the vindictiveness boring into the back of his head.

'Boyd Cameron.'

'Brother?' George asked.

'My brother's son.'

James felt his leg muscles tense. On hearing his name, Boyd edged into the darkest corner.

George went to open the curtains. 'Can we have a bit more light on the subject?'

Miss Cameron rushed across and snatched the drapes from him. 'He's to stay in the darkness.'

Out of her eyeline, George made a face at James, who shrugged at the oddness of it all. He edged toward the darkened corner.

'Boyd, my name is James. You've no need to be frightened. We're not here to scare you or harm you in any way.' He turned to Miss Cameron. 'Does he know what's happened?'

'Of course he knows,' Jeannie replied bitterly. 'He's the cause of it.'

James bit back a feeling of anger. How on earth had this woman become so hateful? He returned to Boyd. 'We're all very sorry about your father. This man here is a policeman. He's a good friend of mine and he has a couple of questions to ask you. Are you happy to answer?'

James' eyes were becoming accustomed to the dimness and he could make out a slight nod.

'Would you like your aunt to sit with you?'

An immediate shake of the head

followed. James raised his eyebrows. That was a telling gesture.

'Would you like to come and sit a little closer?

Another shake of the head.

George joined him in the middle of the room. 'Did you hear anything last night, Boyd?'

Boyd shook his head slowly.

'What did you do during the night? Did you leave the room for any reason?'

James studied what he could make out of the boy. He stood in the corner hugging himself. He was a slight lad and it was difficult to put an age to him. James guessed him to be thirteen or fourteen judging by his stature. His shoulders were yet to develop and he had an awkwardness about him that only boys on the cusp of maturity had.

From what James could make out, he had blond hair and dark, hollow eyes. His clothes hung as if they were two sizes too big. Every question George asked was answered with a nod or a shake of the head. Boyd, it seemed, had been oblivious to any activities during the night.

George tugged James' sleeve and gestured for them to go.

'Boyd,' said James, 'we're going to leave now. But if you think of anything you need to tell us, you let us know. I'll leave our details with your aunt.'

They crept out of the room and Jeannie locked the door. James frowned at her.

'Why on earth are you locking the door?'

'My brother's wishes. Boyd has a routine; it's not to be altered.'

George expressed his own concern over keeping the boy locked in his room. 'I'm sorry Miss Cameron, but that doesn't seem right. You're almost keeping the boy prisoner. Is he dangerous?'

She slipped the keys into her pocket. 'He'll be down once I've prepared dinner. I've to prepare the meal. He's not to be seen.'

James pressed for more information but her thunderous stare stopped him from doing so.

'You'll no' be prying into my affairs. You'll not set foot inside this house again.' She stabbed a finger at George.

'You too. God will punish those who punish us. Lord forgive us.'

The diatribe continued all the way down the stairs until they reached the front door. George picked up his trilby.

'Miss Cameron. You are the one who has accused what appears to be a young boy of murdering his own father. You took us up to that room and allowed us to question him. Don't, therefore, lay down the law with me. If I need to follow this up, I will. I respect your beliefs but don't think, for one minute, that you're not above the law. Good day to you.'

James followed without a word. He hadn't heard George sound so stern for a long time.

On the driveway, he swung his friend round. 'How can that boy have murdered his father? Not only is it an act that fills me with horror, but did you see him? I know it was dark, but he was thin, almost malnourished — all skin and bone. He reminded me of those awful pictures that came out of the concentration camps.'

'If his father was keeping him prisoner, that's a motive for murder.'

'But we're forgetting something.'

'I know. Boyd's door was locked from the outside.'

'Not only that. Christie Cameron's door was locked from the inside.'

'Well then I've got a quandary on my hands.'

'If that boy did murder someone, then he must have the ability to go through sealed doors. But if that was the case, locking him up would hardly deter him.'

George stared at the ground and then gazed along the front wall. The wind had flipped the lid of the dustbin to the ground and a newspaper fluttered as if waiting to take off from its confines. He strode over to retrieve the lid. Before he replaced it, he took out the paper. James wandered over with his hands in his pockets.

'Found something?'

George waved the paper. 'Yesterday's local.' He jabbed it with an index finger.

James examined the article about the escaped convict. It was accompanied by a tiny photograph of a large man with a huge, grey beard and flowing grey locks.

'Any news on him?'

'Nothing,' said George. 'Gone underground. Someone's shielding him.'

James swallowed hard and pictured Bert handing Locksmith Joe a loaf of stale bread. He pushed the thought to the back of his mind and hoped, with all his heart, that his instinct was wrong. George strode toward his car, leaving James to scurry after him.

'Do you think there's foul play here?'

George stroked his chin. 'Need to wait for a medical report.' He tutted at James. 'This is your doing. This sounded like a simple death. The door was locked from the inside. Philip is the same as every other general practitioner: cautious. Collins didn't seem bothered by it.'

James held his tongue. From where he was standing, Collins wasn't bothered by anything and had simply wanted to get back to the station.

His friend groaned. 'Look, I can't say anything more until I get a report.'

'And *my doing* is what?'

'Your confounded curiosity is rubbing off on me.' George gritted his teeth in exasperation. 'I know the doors are locked, but the sister is pointing us to foul play. Normally, I'd dismiss it because it's outrageous and she seems a bit unhinged herself.' He patted James on the back and climbed into his car. 'Give Beth my regards. I'll probably see you at the scarecrow festival in a couple o' days — if I can get some time off, that is.'

The gravel popped as George's car disappeared down the drive. James took one final look at the house. The curtains in the window above twitched and he felt a sense of anger and helplessness settle on his shoulders.

Driving home, he pondered on the life of Boyd Cameron and wondered if he was mentally unstable or a simple boy mistreated by his guardians. And what was Jeannie Cameron's outburst all about? One minute she wanted him 'prying', the next minute he was banished from the house. Either way, he wanted to find out and he knew someone who would be the ideal candidate to coax Boyd from his confines.

8

Later that day, James returned to Cory House with Beth.

'Are you sure we're going to be welcome?' she asked, somewhat anxiously.

'Well, if we're not, we simply walk away,' he replied as they mounted the steps to the front door. 'Although it sounds like suicide, there is some suspicion and Cameron's death intrigues me. But, more importantly, I'm rather concerned about young Boyd.'

His proposal to return had seemed like a splendid idea when he made it; but in the descending mist and drizzle, he wasn't so sure. He'd persuaded Beth to bake Nanna Harrington's gingerbread slices as a peace offering in the hope that this would lower the barriers into the Cameron home. The dampness hanging in the air mirrored his mood. He knocked on the door. After a couple of minutes, Jeannie Cameron turned the key and peered through a small opening.

'You.'

Beth held up a tin. 'We made some gingerbread. For Boyd.'

James put on his most humble face. 'I wanted to apologise if you felt we were being too intrusive, Miss Cameron. We have nothing but yours and Boyd's welfare at heart. Will you allow us a few minutes?'

Miss Cameron scrutinised them, then held the door open. 'You'll be prying, no doubt.'

Beth stared at her in horror, but James put in. 'Not really. My wife wanted to welcome Boyd to the village.' He noted Miss Cameron's stiffness and put his hands up. 'No questions, Miss Cameron. She simply wanted to offer some comfort and support. I promise to stay away if that would put your mind at rest. Allow my wife the courtesy of delivering her gift to young Boyd.'

Jeannie Cameron considered the statement for some time and, although there was no warmth in her response, she retrieved the keys from her apron and handed them to Beth.

'I'll thank you to go straight in and not prowl about.'

As they went upstairs, Beth pulled a face at James. 'Are we not being offered refreshments?' she whispered.

'I believe that would mean inviting us to stay longer than she would like.'

He steered her toward the locked room, took the keyring from her and searched for the appropriate key. On the fourth attempt, he heard the click of the lock. He knocked gently and nudged the door open a fraction.

'Boyd, it's James. We met this morning. I've brought my wife, Beth, along to meet you. She's made some cakes.' He peered around the room to locate him. The boy stood in the shadows at the far wall. 'Are you happy for us to come in?'

Boyd bobbed his head. James opened the door and Beth went in ahead of him. He'd already briefed her on the room, the atmosphere and the frightened soul that would appear before her. He watched as she immediately launched into her plan of action. She chose the sofa an appropriate distance away from Boyd, and beckoned for James to join her. On the side table, she placed the open tin of gingerbread.

'Hello, Boyd. I'm Beth. I've brought some delicious cakes to share with you. They're made to a recipe that belonged to James' grandmother. I do so love to keep her memory alive. And I understand that you're from Yorkshire . . . '

James settled back in the sofa and admired his wife's ability to calm a sensitive situation. She chattered on about all sorts of nonsense and refrained from asking Boyd direct questions. Instead, she supposed he was from Yorkshire; she assumed he had an education; she guessed that he had interests. During the next half an hour, James learnt a great deal.

In a soft northern lilt, the boy quietly disclosed that he was fifteen years old; he'd been educated at home by a tutor; he collected stamps, made models and liked to draw. He was born near Otley and the family had moved to Yorkshire shortly before. Beth spoke of her education in Boston and that she had some American stamps he might like. She described GJ and his artist workshops up at the house.

'I think you two would get along well. Perhaps he could show you some of his drawings.'

She lifted a slice of gingerbread and placed it on a napkin on the table. Boyd hesitated. Placing a slice on the edge of the table, she took a bite of her own.

'Mmm. Moist and full of ginger — just as it should be.' She smiled at Boyd. 'Don't let it go stale.'

Boyd took a step forward and hesitated again as he watched the door. James, now accustomed to the dimness, could see a trace of fear in his stance.

Then he moved into the light. James smiled.

Boyd was an albino with white hair, pale pink eyes and an almost translucent skin. He picked up the gingerbread with slender fingers and sat on the edge of the armchair opposite them. He bit into the cake and ate slowly. His eyes darted from Beth, to James, to the door and back again.

As Beth continued gaining his trust, James took in his surroundings. In contrast to the sparseness of the living room, the walls here were lined with shelves full of books. He saw another table, on which, by the light of several small lamps, Boyd had built a tractor out of Meccano. On the floor by his feet was an airmail envelope. James picked it up and took note of the front. Marked 'Private and Confidential', it was addressed to Boyd, via a lady called Lucy Braithwaite in Hove. It was post-marked Bombay in India. He placed it on the table.

'India,' said James. 'I have a friend who comes from India.'

Boyd's face lit up at the mention of India. He swallowed the last piece of his gingerbread slice and kept his focus on the tin. Beth promised he could keep the cake as she had brought it especially for him. He reached in for another slice.

'My brother lives in India,' he said. His accent was a soft Yorkshire brogue.

James stared at Beth, then at Boyd. 'You have a brother?'

The young boy nodded. 'Calvin. He's ten years older. He left home when I was five.' He gazed into the distance. 'I miss him.'

'Does he come home much?'

'He sends me stamps.' His face brightened. 'He's got a typewriter and I'm going to live with him.'

'That's lovely for you,' said James. After a brief pause, he added, 'Boyd, are you sad that your father has died?'

The young man shrank back in his chair. 'I'm not a bad person. I've done nothing wrong.'

'Why would you think you've done anything wrong, Boyd?'

His gaze fell to the floor. 'She thinks I killed him. I didn't.'

Beth looked horrified. 'Would you prefer that your aunt didn't lock the door?'

Boyd hugged himself and nodded.

James' heart went out to Beth. She was clearly upset for the boy. He patted her hand. 'I say, would you like to come to the scarecrow festival? Perhaps, if you want to, we can show you around the village and introduce you to GJ.'

Boyd stared at the door.

James stood up and helped Beth to her feet. He moved closer to Boyd and realised how slight he was. James wasn't a stocky man, but he felt like a giant next to this frail figure. The fact that his clothes hung so loose didn't help matters. The only things that really fitted him were his shoes. They were terribly scuffed and he'd painted pictures of faces on the toes.

'Let's see if we can talk your aunt into letting you go,' he said gently. 'She can't keep you locked in here all day. In the meantime, enjoy your gingerbread.'

Beth reached over to hold the young man's hands. 'Would you like to come to the scarecrow festival?'

The boy's face brightened but on hearing the door open, he scurried to the far corners of his room.

'Will ye no' leave us in peace ... ' began Jeannie Cameron, filling the door-frame.

'Of course,' replied James forcing himself to be pleasant. 'We're so sorry to have taken up your time.'

They bade a fond farewell to Boyd, promised to visit again, and made their way down to the hall, where James retrieved his hat and gloves from the table.

'I say, Miss Cameron, he's a splendid chap, young Boyd. I'm not sure that you need to keep him marooned in his room all day.'

'You'll mind your business and not be prying into mine. I know he's to blame,' she snarled. 'I shouldnae sleep under this roof.'

'What about Calvin — will he come home for the funeral?'

If eyes could spit venom, James was sure he'd be dead on the spot. She snatched open the front door.

'You've done your prying, now leave me in peace.'

The door slammed behind them.

'Well, well,' said James trotting down the steps. 'We hit a nerve there.'

Beth marched ahead of him and turned. 'James, I can't bear the thought of leaving that poor boy up there.'

He put an arm around her shoulder and kissed the top of her head. 'I know, darling, but let's think this through. We can't go kidnapping him. Even if we did, what would we do with him?'

'Give him a life, show him some love

and affection. That's what we'd do.'

He unlocked the car and held the passenger door open for her. 'Let's have a chat with Stephen. Perhaps George may have some ideas. I wonder if Calvin will be back for the funeral.'

'You know, if that man had an overdose of a sleeping draught then I think she's the more likely suspect,' said Beth. 'After all, they say that poison is a woman's preferred method of murder.'

She slammed the door shut. James observed the bedroom window and saw the curtain twitch. He waved. A pale hand waved back. Beth was right. Poison was a woman's killing tool. But was it the sleeping draught, or was that slight bruising Jackson mentioned indicative of something more sinister?

9

Locksmith Joe shuffled through the wooded glade to his makeshift home; a selection of wooden slats nailed together with a ragged piece of oily tarpaulin thrown over. The air smelt damp. Soggy leaves on the forest floor made his joints ache and he silently longed for an armchair and roaring log fire. His stomach groaned and he realised it was several hours since he'd eaten.

The escape plan had gone without a hitch, but he'd not thought so far ahead. Where to live, how to eat, who to rely on and who to trust? He couldn't go home. That was the first place the coppers would look. No, he had to stay here in Cavendish. The only mate he knew was here; the only bloke he could trust — so this was where he came.

Branches snapped. He jumped, squinted into the trees then scurried under the timbers and peered out. His heart slowed as he saw the jaunty figure of Bert Briggs tread a path toward him.

'Oi, oi. How's it going?' He tossed a sack onto the leaves.

'I'm bloody starving, mate. You got anything to eat?'

Bert pushed his flat cap back, delved into the sack and brought out bread, cheese, milk and ham. Joe grabbed the lot and tore the end off the loaf. From inside his jacket, Bert pulled out a Thermos flask and waved it at him.

'Vegetable soup.' He nestled the flask in the leaves. 'Make it last. I can't get back to you till tomorrow morning. There's a blanket at the bottom o' the sack.'

'You're a diamond, Bert. Thanks.'

Bert scanned the woods. 'Yeah, well, it's what mates do, but you can't stay 'ere. This is all part of an estate and Lord 'arrington's one of me best mates. We'll have to find somewhere else. Why come 'ere, anyway? Your family's down at Bognor.'

Joe flicked crumbs from his beard. 'Following someone, ain't I? And this is where they are. And you're the only mate I can trust around here.'

Bert grimaced and scratched his head. 'Remember, one night only. Don't make a noise and don't light a fire.'

'Who's this Lord 'arrington bloke?'

Bert leant over him. 'Don't mess on your own doorstep, Joe. Or more importantly, don't mess on mine. You target 'im, I back off. Understood?'

Joe held his hands up in surrender. 'Just asking, mate. I'm not gonna do him over, am I? I'm not about to get myself nicked when I've got so close.' He broke off a piece of Cheddar. 'Don't you wanna know what I've come 'ere for?'

'No, mate. The less I know, the less mixed up I am.' He gently kicked Joe's calf. 'I'll be back tomorrow.'

'Bring us a full English, will yer?' Joe grinned.

'You'll get your full English when you've done what you 'ave to do.' Bert trudged away.

★ ★ ★

James and Beth strolled toward the vicarage, where Anne stood on the doorstep waiting to invite them in.

'I heard your car draw up — dead on time as usual. You must have an inbuilt clock in your head.'

James took off his cap and thanked his schooldays for his timekeeping ability.

'Woe betide you if you arrived late for lessons. I learnt pretty sharp that punctuality put me in people's good books and it's stayed with me ever since.'

'And anyway,' Beth put in, 'it's good manners to arrive on time.'

Anne showed them through to the front room where Stephen was slicing a lemon drizzle sponge. On the sofa opposite were GJ and Catherine, looking like love's young dream. GJ leapt to his feet.

'I'm so pleased you both could make it! It means a great deal. Catherine, of course, knows how wonderful you've been to me over the last year. I asked Bert here too but he couldn't make it.'

Catherine cut an attractive yet homely figure and she gushed in her praise of James, Beth and the Merryweathers. 'I can't believe that everyone would put themselves to such trouble for a homeless man, but you did. If you hadn't have done that, I'd never have met GJ at all.'

James flopped onto a sofa, feeling good about himself. 'Surprising where fate leads us, isn't it? A seemingly invisible thread of events that pulls us to where we should be.'

'G-goodness,' said Stephen, 'that's a v-very philosophical and wise statement. I believe I should consider that for a sermon.'

Anne joined him on the sofa as he jotted a couple of words down on a notepad. She poured tea from a beautiful bone china tea pot patterned with swirling blue and yellow lines. Beth was quick to compliment it.

'A present from my grandmother,' Anne said. 'It was given to her and she's never used it. She doesn't like the design. Too modern.'

'I like these modern designs,' replied Beth. She turned to Catherine. 'Have you started your bottom drawer?'

Catherine gave a coy smile. 'I have, yes. There's not much in it at the moment, but we know our families are giving us things they don't use much.' She held

GJ's hand. 'We're fortunate that GJ already has a home so we've a good start. Much better than most couples.'

James thanked Anne for his slice of sponge. 'Well, I'm sure that whatever you collect will be useful.'

'We've some towels you can have,' said Beth. 'I always seem to have a huge amount of those.'

'You're all very kind,' said GJ. 'I can't believe I deserve such generosity from people I've only known since the spring.'

'Nonsense,' said James. 'There are some people who make an impression on us as soon as we meet them. You, GJ, are one of those people.'

Stephen scribbled on his notepad. 'Th-that's another I can use. Have you been r-reading philosophy or something?'

James said that it was an interest and turned the conversation back to the couple, asking when the wedding would be. GJ smoothed back his thick, blond hair and let Catherine answer.

'We thought we'd marry this December.'

Anne clapped her hands and announced that it was a wonderful time of year. Beth agreed and asked if they meant Christmas Day itself.

'No, no,' said GJ. 'We thought about the first of December. I've been able to get permission for us to marry here and our respective families are fine with that.'

'Is your aunt coming?'

GJ's wonderful smile surfaced as he announced that Juliet Brooks-Hunter would be attending. Also on the invitation list were his late mother's friend and confidant, Kushal Patel, along with Gladys Smith and her son and daughter-in-law, David and Nancy from the East End mission.

'Oh splendid,' said James. He turned to Stephen. 'You know, if you want to have some good philosophy quotes, you should spend an hour with Mr Patel.'

Mr Patel had assisted James during his investigation into the death of an elderly spinster in the village.

'I-I look forward to it,' said Stephen as he reached for his diary. He flicked through the pages. 'The 1st of December is free. Shall we say three o'clock?'

GJ held Catherine's hand. 'Three o'clock is fine.' The young man turned to

James and appeared to be plucking up some courage. 'I wonder, Lord Harrington, if you would be my best man?'

Pride filled James. It was as if his own son had asked him the question. He realised, then, how fond he'd become of the chap. He placed his cup and saucer down and held out his hand. 'I'd be honoured to, GJ.'

Beth and Anne asked about bridesmaids and dresses. Catherine expressed some doubt about who could make them as her mother had difficulty sewing due to an injury she had sustained during the war.

'She helped out in a munitions factory and damaged the fingers of her right hand. She's all right, but intricate stuff like sewing . . . well, she struggles.'

Beth empathised with her. 'That mustn't spoil your plans. You and your mother choose the material and the patterns and Anne and I will make them.'

Catherine beamed in relief and went through her visions for the day itself. She spoke with an excitement that soon transferred itself to Beth and Anne as they *oohed* and *aahed* over ideas. GJ was happy to ride the carousel of enthusiasm. Stephen made an appointment to discuss the reading of the banns and hymns. Once the discussions and suggestions had died down, James whispered something in Beth's ear. She listened intently and gave an encouraging nod. He turned to the young couple.

'I say, do you two have arrangements for a party afterwards?'

GJ said that they had discussed it but weren't sure whether they could really afford it. 'I know we're better off than most people, but an artist's wage is not the best so I don't want to be too extravagant. Catherine's family struggle. She lost her dad during the war. We thought about drinks back at my house. It's only small, as you know, but we could manage. Just the closest of friends and relatives.'

James remembered the cottage well, but the rooms were tiny and they would be challenged to accommodate everyone.

'Will you allow us to throw you something? You don't have to say yes; it may not sit well with you, but consider it our wedding present to you both. We generally have a rather lovely setting at Harrington's over the Christmas period and we always kick the month off with a dinner and dance. We can put a side room by for your guests but you'll have to share the dance floor with the residents.'

Catherine almost wept for joy as she brought her hands to her face.

'I think that means we're saying yes,' said GJ.

The chatter continued for some time. Although Beth and Anne were more than happy to share their knowledge and suggestions concerning arrangements, James and Stephen made the excuse of wanting some fresh air and left the group to continue chatting about their plans and possible honeymoon destinations.

They found themselves heading toward the church. Inside, James rubbed his hands together as Stephen straightened hymn books and cushions.

'A-any news on Cory House?'

Sitting on the front pew, James outlined everything that had happened to date: the mystery of the locked doors; Jeannie Cameron's erratic behaviour, and the condition of the lad, Boyd. Stephen gazed up at a white marble carving of Jesus on the cross.

'For s-such a God-fearing man, I cannot h-help but think that Mr Cameron did not appear to have treated his son well.'

'Sons, plural.'

Stephen stood rooted to the spot. 'At the house?'

James explained that the elder brother was in India. 'Ten years older and left when Boyd was five. Hasn't been back since, which leads me to believe that he couldn't wait to get out himself.'

The vicar stared at the ceiling. Ancient oak beams criss-crossed above him. 'How did you f-find out about him?'

'The brothers remain in contact. You should have seen the look on Boyd's face when I noticed the letter. An anticipation: like a child on Christmas Day. And when I mentioned that I knew someone from India, I thought he was going to hug me.'

Stephen turned to face him. 'Your f-friend Mr Patel . . . from your description of him, I believe he could be of great help to Boyd.'

'Yes, I wondered that. If anyone can gain his trust and give him some confidence, he can. What's happening about Cameron's funeral — have you been asked to conduct it?'

'F-fortunately, no. I-I say fortunately because I feel I would never m-meet Miss Cameron's expectations. The funeral is yet to be arranged, but I have suggested that I r-remember him in prayers this Sunday and she agreed to attend.'

'Goodness, you are honoured. You didn't convince her to attend the scarecrow festival.'

The vicar shuddered. 'I-I wouldn't dare. Do you th-think Boyd would like to come?'

James thought Boyd would dearly love to come. 'But the likelihood of me prising him away from the mad aunt is remote.'

'Shame.'

The tip-tap of heels prompted both men to turn. Beth walked toward them with her coat on. She carried James' jacket and hat. 'Here you are. We're needed at Cory House.'

James frowned. 'Oh?'

'It's just George being cautious. Jeannie

Cameron apparently called him earlier screaming blue murder at him and telling him he should do his job and arrest Boyd.'

'Oh, for goodness' sake, what on earth's the matter with the woman?' muttered James as he shrugged his jacket on. 'What does he need us for?'

'Boyd has barricaded the door,' said Beth. 'George wanted to take some fingerprints. I think that's more to convince Miss Cameron that he's innocent rather than gather evidence. But Boyd's now frightened to death and won't let anyone in.' She gave him a cheesy grin. 'Except us.'

James smiled. 'D'you want to join us, Stephen?'

'I-I'll leave you to it. I-I'm sure you'll do a splendid job. I shall see you at the festival tomorrow. Let's hope that will be less traumatic.'

James followed Beth down the aisle with thoughts nagging at him. Was Christie Cameron murdered? Until the coroner's report came through, he couldn't be sure. If it was Boyd who was responsible, how on earth did he get through two locked doors? Why was Jeannie Cameron so convinced of his guilt? Or was she pointing suspicion away from herself? After all, in his brief meeting with the Cameron siblings, she appeared to have been his skivvy. Had she tired of his bullying ways and killed him herself? Getting rid of Boyd would leave her with an independence she might never have known before.

'No,' he mumbled, 'that can't be right.'

'What's that, sweetie?'

'If Jeannie Cameron killed her brother, why shout about murder when suicide is a possible verdict?'

She playfully punched him as they headed for the car. 'You're not going into mystery mode, are you?'

He couldn't hide his crooked grin as he unlocked the door. 'Do you know, Beth, I think I am.'

10

Bob Tanner and the Taverners belted out a continuous stomping hornpipe on a selection of concertinas and melodeons as they led the scarecrow parade along the high street and toward the village green. Following behind were the local Morris team dancing in time, their bells jangling and handkerchiefs waving. Boys and girls skipped alongside them and villagers and visitors lined the streets to clap and stamp along to the infectious rhythm. Residents with houses along the route waved from upstairs windows and specially-made 'scarecrow' flags flapped in the breeze from every available lamp-post. High in the sky swallows dipped and dived as if in time with the music.

Twenty-five scarecrows kept up with the Morris team, all of them from the village or surrounding farms and each one vying for the title of Best Scarecrow. There had been no rules concerning how the costumes should look and the result was a variety of imaginative figures that enthralled the onlookers.

To the delight of the children, Dr Philip Jackson and his wife, Helen, skipped along as fictional scarecrows, Worzel Gummidge and Aunt Sally. Philip had fixed a most realistic parsnip on his nose and wore a wig of straw, while Helen wore a beautiful bonnet and had painted her cheeks a bright rosy red. Their daughter, Natasha, copied her mum's costume and had blacked out a front tooth.

A number of farmhands had created costumes from old sacking filled with straw, leaving small trails of hay in their wakes. Others had transformed themselves into popular cartoon characters, such as Popeye, Olive Oyl and Betty Boop. Charlie Hawkins, the librarian, was hardly recognisable under his Long John Silver disguise and mad solicitor, Mr Bateson, had dressed as Davy Crockett with a dandy fur hat.

They came in all shapes and sizes, shaking hands with villagers on the pavements as they skipped from one side of the road to the other; the pounding beat of the music continuing.

A couple of the younger farmhands had opted for rather scary costumes featuring masks with haunted expressions and long, spindly fingers. They took great delight in chasing young children, who screamed their lungs out as they sprinted to the safety of their laughing parents' sides.

James, dressed in a light tweed jacket and brown corduroy trousers, was ahead of the procession and made his way to the green to await its arrival. He stood by the entrance to the marquee.

The encounter at Cory House the previous evening had gone amicably. He'd convinced George to delay pushing Boyd for fingerprints and suggested that this be requested after everyone had slept on it. George had, to his surprise, agreed and was quick to depart, muttering something about Jeannie Cameron being as mad as a March hare. He had to agree. There was something quite unhinged about the woman. One minute she was screaming murder, the next they were accused of causing trouble and being told to mind their own business.

The band came into view. James stood

tall and anticipated another successful festival ahead of them. He peered into the marquee.

'I say, everyone, the parade's coming.'

A damp mist had descended on proceedings but, as was always the case, this didn't curb people's enthusiasm. The ladies of the Women's Institute had done themselves proud by making the marquee a welcoming finish to proceedings. Coloured light bulbs were dotted across the canopy and red, white and blue bunting draped from the support poles to the marquee walls. Along the back wall of the tent stood rows of trestle tables loaded with cakes, pies, pickles and breads. At one end was a makeshift stage and, at the other, Donovan and Kate Delaney, proprietors of the Half Moon, had set up a bar. Just along from the entrance was Graham's traditional hog roast and James was already salivating as the smell of pork and crackling reached him.

Prizes for the best scarecrows were safely lodged at the back of the stage. They consisted of a box of tea and biscuits, courtesy of Elsie Taylor who owned the café between Cavendish and the neighbouring village, Charnley; a leg of lamb, donated by Graham Porter; and a small hamper from Fortnum and Mason, donated by James and Beth, as first prize.

As the noise of the parade increased, organisers spilled out of the marquee to watch the scarecrows dance around the green. With no break in the music, the hornpipes turned to jigs and reels as they made their way across the grass. Several members of the folk club walked alongside the Taverners with their own melodeons to provide a rousing finale. Tommy Hawkins, the librarian's son, rushed to join them and accompanied the beat on his toy drum.

James felt Beth's hand in his. 'Oh James, what a colourful scene.'

'Isn't it?' James replied as the vibrant and energetic scarecrows danced past them. 'They seem to get more creative as each year goes by.'

After one circuit of the green, Bob Tanner led them into the marquee and, on their heels, the Morris team, the scarecrows and, finally, the villagers who had previously lined the streets. The junior school choir, led by Mr Chrichton, immediately launched into their prepared song:

'Oats and beans and barley grow,
Oats and beans and barley grow
Can you or I or anyone know how
oats and beans and barley grow.'

'How w-wonderful to see the fl-flock together and enjoying the day,' Stephen observed as he watched the crowd disperse to the various refreshment tables.

Anne joined them. 'I think it's wonderful that you keep these traditions alive.'

James ushered them in to the centre of the marquee. 'Villages are not villages unless we have a community, and the only way to do that is ensure we keep our folklore alive. However, I'm not entirely sure that scarecrows are much to do with folklore. But, like you say, Anne, it's a wonderful spectacle.'

Donovan attempted to sway James to have a pint of Autumn Gold but James declined. 'I will partake of your finest ale later. It's a little early for me and, if I'm being honest, I could really fancy a nice cup of tea.'

Beth, Stephen and Anne agreed that tea would be most welcome. Assuring Donovan of their custom later in the day, they weaved their way through the crowds to the corner where Elsie had set up a mini version of her café.

'Ah, hello Elsie,' said James. 'This is rather splendid.'

Elsie Taylor, a buxom woman in her mid-thirties, had duplicated her café as best she could with red and white checked tablecloths and white wooden chairs with dimpled cushions tied in place. Her counter consisted of an empty beer barrel for the cash register, a calor gas stove and two planks of wood for preparation. Elsie invited them to take the last available table.

'I'm pleased with it, I must say. I'm doing teas only, I'm afraid. Don't want to step on the WI's toes, but I'm quite happy if you want to get something from there and eat it here.'

Beth suggested they treat themselves to Mrs Keates' award-winning Victoria sponge. Stephen leapt up and insisted he order and pay for them. In a few moments, they were sipping tea and enjoying feather-light cake with raspberry jam and butter-cream filling.

Around them, villagers, scarecrows and organisers took full advantage of the refreshments. The parade had begun early and, by the time everyone had reached the marquee, stomachs were rumbling, especially when they saw the delights on offer. Through the crowd, James spotted George with a hog-roast roll clasped in his hand. Alongside him, GJ and Catherine were speaking to two young ladies that he didn't recognise, so he presumed they were visitors who had come to see the parade.

Rose and Lilac Crumb, the Snoop Sisters, scurried up to him. James felt his mood change. Their presence meant one thing — gossip.

Stephen greeted them. 'Ah l-ladies, how wonderful to see you.'

'Mm,' replied Rose.

'I'm sure,' Lilac put in.

James wondered if they ever went anywhere separately. He'd never actually seen them apart at any time. Rose sidled up to him.

'She's 'ere.'

He frowned. 'Who?'

Lilac's thumb signalled behind her. 'The grieving widow.'

James shifted in his chair to get a better idea of who the sisters were speaking of. All he could see was Bert having what appeared to be an amusing chat with Graham about an elongated piece of crackling.

'Not there,' Lilac said. 'There.'

James froze. Standing at the entrance of the marquee was Jeannie Cameron. 'Good Lord!'

Beth followed his gaze. Her jaw dropped. Stephen and Anne both rose and dashed over to welcome her.

Beth frowned at James. 'What on earth is she doing here?'

Rose huffed. 'Can't be the grieving widow — coming to a festival.'

Lilac echoed her sister's statement.

James forced a smile. 'Ladies, she was the sister, not the wife.' He jerked a head at their trestle table. 'You have customers.'

They scurried away and Beth gave a disapproving shake of the head. 'Goodness, I do find those women most rude at times.'

'Ye . . . es.' His thoughts were more on Miss Cameron than the Snoop Sisters. She stood by the entrance of the marquee, wearing a dull brown coat. Pinched and upright, she was listening to whatever Anne was saying. 'But, like you say, darling. What on earth is she doing here?'

On James' visits to Cory House, she and her brother had made it quite clear that this festival would not be graced by their presence. The very idea of it appeared to horrify them. Was Jeannie more open to socialising than her brother would have had them think? He had no further time to ponder as the Merryweathers were escorting her toward them.

James and Beth stood to greet her. Stephen pulled a chair out where she sat upright with both hands on her handbag, her wool coat buttoned to the neck. She had the appearance of someone who would not be staying. James asked Elsie for some more tea. He took out a cigarette.

'I must admit, Miss Cameron, I'm somewhat surprised to see you here.'

'I was in the village.' Her hollow eyes looked past James as if searching for something, or someone.

The villagers chatted and laughed and children raced to and fro playing tag. Dorothy Forbes patted the microphone on the stage. Piercing feedback through the speaker caused everyone to grimace.

James chuckled. 'That's one way to quieten everyone down.'

'Hello. Hello, can you all hear me?' The villagers gathered. 'The voting for the scarecrows has finished and the counting is taking place as we speak. We should have the results through in the next five minutes.'

James noticed Dorothy's aloof stare at his friend, Bert. It didn't matter what the occasion was, Bert dressed as Bert. He could have been mistaken as one of the scarecrows in his shabby tweed jacket, baggy trousers and flat cap.

Beth nudged him and drew his attention to Jeannie Cameron, whose complexion was as white as chalk. Her eyes narrowed and scanned the crowd. James followed her gaze. Everyone was facing the stage with the exception of one man; a large, bulky individual with a bobble hat, a wool coat and scuffed boots. He had thick, wiry hair curling from under his hat and an unruly beard. When James turned his attention back to Jeannie, she was already making her way out. James looked across at the man again but he'd disappeared. His eyes searched the crowd. Where on earth did he go?

Beth shrugged his concern away and hinted that he was making too much of things.

Dorothy cleared her throat. 'Lord Harrington asked that Professor Wilkins announce this year's winners. Professor, if you don't mind putting your drink down.' She pushed the microphone away. 'It doesn't come across as very professional.'

Professor Wilkins mounted the stage with his pint firmly in his grip. Dorothy looked on with disapproval as he held up his glass. She turned on her heels and marched off.

James grinned, eased back in his chair and folded his arms in anticipation. It made a change to sit back and enjoy someone else's speech.

'Right,' said the Professor. 'I'm not

going to speak for too long. I'm sure you're all keen to enjoy the food and music.'

'Here, here,' shouted a scarecrow.

He settled the crowd down. 'Lord Harrington asked that I tell you a little about scarecrows while the votes are counted.' He took a sip of his pint. 'Although not an ancient English tradition, scarecrows are part of our folklore. They began life here around the 15th century in medieval Britain. In those days, we had young lads who'd run around throwing stones at birds to startle them. But, when the Great Plague came a couple of hundred years later, farmers couldn't find enough lads to do the job. So, the scarecrow we know and love today was born — a sack stuffed with straw with a turnip face.'

He took another slurp and Dorothy made to mount the stage, but Wilkins continued. Dorothy walked away with a huff. James stifled a grin — underneath his gruff exterior, the Professor had an underrated sense of humour. The man knew Dorothy wanted him off.

'Gradually, over time, the scarecrow has taken a life of its own. As you can see here, the costumes are worthy of a Cavendish Players production.' Dorothy softened. 'And, children, you'll notice that the scarecrows in the fields often have wooden clappers and tin cans hanging from them to rattle in the wind. They've taken the place of sticks and stones. So, not much has changed since those early days.'

He raised his pint to the crowd who applauded politely. Dorothy handed him a slip of paper.

'Right you are. We had twenty-five entries this year.'

A young lad standing to the side of James tugged at his dad's sleeve. 'No there weren't,' James heard him say. 'There were twenty-six. I counted 'em.'

Wilkins continued. 'In third place and winning the leg of lamb is the Popeye scarecrow.' He checked his notes. 'Underneath that costume is a gentleman called Kevin who helps out on Tolly Farm.'

A huge cheer rang out as Kevin made his way to the side of the stage to collect his prize.

'Racing into second place and worthy winners of Elsie's box of tea and biscuits is a family venture, Worzel Gummidge, Aunt Sally and miniature Sally. Cavendish's very own doctor, Philip Jackson, his wife, Helen, and their beautiful daughter, Natasha.'

Another cheer rang around the marquee as the Jacksons collected their prize.

'And first prize, a wonderful Fortnum and Mason hamper, goes to our librarian, Charlie Hawkins for his Long John Silver scarecrow. Added to this is a cash donation of five pounds.'

Tommy and Susan Hawkins yelled with excitement. James felt satisfied with the result. Everyone in the marquee warmly applauded the choice. Charlie Hawkins always struggled for the necessities of life. A widower, who had lost his wife to pneumonia soon after their children were born, was hugely popular in the village. Tommy and Susan were Charlie's life and James knew the cash would go toward a family treat.

The boy to the side of James followed his dad toward the makeshift bar, still asserting the fact that there were twenty-six scarecrows, not twenty-five.

'H-he's sure of himself, i-isn't he?' said Stephen, who had also heard the conversation.

Anne gathered the empty plates together. 'He's in Luke's class at school. I understand he's good at counting, so his adding up is probably accurate.'

They meandered over to the side of the marquee to view the baking competition winners on the WI table as Dorothy announced that Mr Bateson would sing his specially-written scarecrow song. True to form, the mad solicitor made use of his wiry frame, wild hair and rubber-faced expressions to turn proceedings into a hilarious piece of entertainment. The children warmed to him and sprinted toward the front to watch his show.

'I'm a scarecrow through the day,
    with my clothes all full of hay,
I've a clapper and tin of stones to
    ring.
I've a carrot on my nose, and I shout
    at all the crows,

So the farmer, he can bring the harvest in.'

Bateson prowled around the marquee singing his song, bewitching the audience with his acting skills as he wove his scarecrow tale. Bob Tanner picked up his guitar and stepped in behind Bateson to accompany him.

Outside, a child screamed. James winced as the high-pitched yell hit his eardrums.

Graham winced. 'That sounds like one of mine. Georgina's got into habit of screaming at the least little thing. No doubt Thomas is teasing her or something.'

Sarah, his wife, handed her drink to Graham. 'I'll go.'

James chuckled. 'It never fails to amaze me how much noise one child can make.'

Anne agreed. 'It's a wonder we don't all go deaf after a few years with your children. They can't seem to do anything quietly. I know our two can't.'

James heard Sarah shouting at the children and ordering them back to the marquee.

Graham pulled a face. 'Blimey, I wonder

115

what they've been up to? Sarah don't normally get that annoyed with 'em.'

Sarah appeared at the entrance of the tent, her face drained of colour. As one, James, Beth, Graham and the Merryweathers hastened toward her. Graham's hands held her face.

'What's up, love? You look like you've seen a ghost.'

Her worried expressed settled on James. 'It's that Cameron woman.' Her eyes shifted to the entrance of the marquee and back again. 'In the shrubs, at the side of the pub.'

James grabbed Stephen and the pair of them rushed toward the Half Moon where Mark, Stephen's eldest son, stood on the pavement, looking into the bushes.

'Mark!' shouted Stephen. 'G-go to your mother.'

Mark raced past them and into the marquee. James and Stephen stopped where the shrubs began. A pair of legs, with black stockings and flat black shoes, stuck out. James inched closer and pulled the branches to one side. Staring back at him was Jeannie Cameron.

11

'I-is she dead?'

James felt for a pulse. 'Yes. And, judging by the marks around her neck, I'd say she was strangled.'

As news spread, the villagers began to spill out onto the green and a buzz of chatter began. What had happened? Had there been an accident? Was it true that Thomas and Georgina had discovered a body? They stood a polite distance away as George reverted to his official standing of Detective Chief Inspector and bent over the body. Philip Jackson, looking comical in his Worzel Gummidge costume, joined them and examined Jeannie Cameron's neck, moving her head gently from side to side. James stood behind him.

'Am I right in believing she was strangled?' he asked.

Philip got to his feet and tugged his parsnip nose off. 'I'd say so, yes.' He caught George's eye. 'I didn't even realise she was here; didn't think it was her sort of thing.'

George sought out confirmation from James, who ran his hands through his hair.

'We thought so, too, but she pitched up around half an hour ago. She joined us at Elsie's little café thing in the corner there but only stayed a couple of minutes. Didn't even drink her tea.'

'And what was she doing here?' asked George.

'Said she was in the village.'

'That's it?'

'That's it,' James said with a frown which prompted George to probe for his thoughts.

'There was a moment where she went deathly white,' continued James. 'I looked across to see what she'd seen. I saw a man.'

'Description?'

James searched his memory. 'Large, bulky, bobble hat, big overcoat and boots. Oh, and a beard.' He met George's stare. 'I couldn't tell you colours, I'm afraid although it all seemed rather drab. His eyes startled me, though.'

George tilted his head.

'Fierce. Not hate — I think that's too strong. It was as if he meant business — that's the only way I can describe it. I couldn't tell you if it was that convict, Locksmith Joe, but it did cross my mind. But why would he kill Jeannie Cameron?'

George retrieved his pipe from his pocket. 'All I can tell you is that he is a killer. The only information I've got about him is that he strangled someone. That's why he was banged up for life.'

'Any reason why he wasn't hanged?'

His friend said that he was waiting for more information. 'I requested it once I heard he was in the area, but somehow they forgot to send it to me. And now it's even more important, especially if he's responsible for this.'

George jotted a few comments down in his notebook. Meanwhile, two constables parked their car on the green, followed closely by an ambulance. George dished out several instructions concerning photographing the crime scene, cordoning the area off, taking statements and removing the body.

James, who'd been joined by Beth, moved to one side and beckoned George over.

'I know you don't like me interfering an' all, but a couple of things struck me as odd.'

'Go on.'

'First, Jeannie Cameron would never come into Cavendish. If she went shopping, it was known that she preferred Haywards Heath. The local shopkeepers never spoke of her gracing them with her presence. So why did she suddenly appear here today, especially so soon after her brother's death?'

'And at a festival she wanted nothing to do with,' Beth put in.

'Second, this casts a good deal of doubt on Christie Cameron. Two deaths, a brother and sister, in the space of three days.'

'There's something else, too,' said Beth. 'We overheard something that I guess may be nothing.' She hesitated, but George encouraged her to speak up.

'Well, we overheard a young boy earlier. He'd counted twenty-six scarecrows.'

'I'd forgotten all about that,' said James.

George shrugged as if to say 'So?'

'There were twenty-five entrants,' said Beth.

Their friend grimaced. 'He could've counted 'em wrong.'

'He could have,' said James. 'But supposing he didn't?'

'Did either of you see anyone take photographs?' asked George.

James shrugged. 'I didn't see anyone in particular, but people do. Memento of the day and all that. There are a few people here who own cameras and Timothy, the local reporter, is about somewhere.'

George called a constable across and instructed him to ask for camera film when taking statements. 'You never know, we may have some pictures of this mystery scarecrow.'

A young lady with short, wavy hair and an impish face skipped forward. James recognised her as one of the ladies in conversation with GJ and Catherine. He put her at around fifteen or sixteen years old. She wore blue jeans, a gold jumper, bobby socks and saddle shoes. She had no qualms about looking at the body in front of her and called out towards the crowd, 'It is her. I told you.'

George cleared his throat. 'Young lady.'

The girl turned with a breezy smile. 'I'm not sorry she's dead. She was a horrid, horrid woman. Her brother was, too.'

James stopped himself from berating the girl for being inappropriate. The other lady that GJ was speaking to emerged from the crowd. James decided she was in her mid-twenties. She stood tall for a woman; around five foot ten, with long blonde hair tied back in a ponytail. She wore a bottle green dress with a chic black cape and held a small purse in her hand. Coming up to James and the others, she pulled the girl aside.

'Suzie, for goodness' sake.'

'I'm only telling the truth. That's what the police want you to do. Isn't that true, Inspector?'

'It's Detective Chief Inspector, young

lady,' replied George. 'And you are?'

The elder one held a hand out. 'I'm Lucy Braithwaite. This is my younger sister, Suzie.'

James recognised the name. Lucy Braithwaite was the lady who'd received the letters to pass on to Boyd.

George steered everyone away from the scene. 'And what do you mean, Suzie, by saying that you're not sorry she's dead?'

The young lady pushed her shoulders back. 'Just what I said. I hated her and that rotten brother of hers, too. If someone did her in, then she deserved it.'

'Suzie, that's quite enough,' said Lucy. 'I'm so sorry, Detective Chief Inspector. My sister is rather immature and doesn't appreciate the gravity of the situation.'

Suzie crossed her arms and turned to George. 'I do appreciate it,' she said brightly. 'I just choose to be truthful about it, not act as if I care when I don't.'

James introduced himself and Beth and asked who they were in relation to the deceased. Suzie started to answer, but Lucy gripped her arm firmly and demanded she stay quiet.

'We're Christie Cameron's nieces. His wife, Auntie Gwen, was our father's sister.'

George emptied his pipe. 'Right. I'm not having this discussion here. I want you two down the station to answer some questions. Give me five minutes and we'll drive you down.'

Suzie fluttered her eyelids. 'I hope you're going to give us a lift home.' She shrugged off another admonishment from Lucy, who continued talking with George.

The young girl turned to James. 'I heard you look into things.'

'I beg your pardon?'

She outlined the brief dialogue she'd had with GJ and Catherine. 'He said how good you were to him and how you solved his mystery. He said you've solved other things, too. Is that true?'

James gave her a knowing look. 'I'm not the police, Miss Braithwaite.'

She checked her watch. 'We live in Hove, but could I speak with you? Would you mind?'

James gave her a card. 'Our details are on here.'

Suzie accepted it with a grateful smile.

'Thank you so much. I know we're strangers, but would you please do something for me?'

James tilted his head in question.

'They'll lay blame and that's not fair.'

'Lay blame?'

George rejoined them.

'Sir?' An ambulance man nearby, who was covering up the body, held a hand out to George. 'Set o' house keys, sir.'

James and Beth gasped in unison. 'Boyd!'

12

In spite of George's resistance, two cars pulled up outside Cory House. The first was a police car driven by George accompanied by one constable and the two nieces. The second was the Jaguar with James, Beth, Stephen and Anne. George mounted the steps to the front door and stared at the numerous keys. Lucy peered over his shoulder and picked out the correct one.

Opening the door, Suzie raced up the stairs and hammered on Boyd's door. 'Boyd, it's Suzie. Are you all right?'

Lucy followed up at a gentler pace. George, having instructed the constable to stay by the door, scrutinised James and his entourage.

'And why are you here?'

'Oh, George,' said Beth, 'we can get more out of Boyd than you can — you need us here.'

'A-Anne and I are h-here in our official capacity,' added Stephen. 'Lending faith and s-support to a young — '

'Yes, all right,' George blustered.

On the landing, Suzie demanded that Boyd be set free. Lucy's glare resulted in her sister apologising to George. Having selected the correct key, he unlocked the door. Suzie burst in and rushed to the young man. James was surprised at the length of the embrace and the emotion behind it. George cleared his throat and addressed Lucy.

'Does Boyd have a set of keys?'

'No. They kept him hidden from the world; wouldn't let him see the light of day.' Her lips tightened. 'Suzie was right, you know. They were horrid people. How could a father do that to his own son?'

George took his notebook out. 'He always kept him locked up?'

'More so since Auntie Gwen died. He blamed Auntie Gwen.'

'For what?'

'For what Boyd is. An albino. Uncle Christie felt it was some sort of punishment. He didn't see him as normal. The wrath of God and all that nonsense.' Lucy held a hand to her forehead and swung

127

round to Stephen. 'I'm so sorry, I didn't mean it like that. It's just that he became so strict about his faith. Not like you. Oh goodness, you know what I mean, don't you?'

Stephen's warm smile settled her. 'I-I know exactly what you mean.'

'Mr Cameron wasn't terribly forgiving of us, either,' Anne added.

'Boyd is such a wonderfully kind individual,' continued Lucy. 'He wouldn't say boo to a goose and he certainly has no malice in him.' She clutched George's arm. 'It will destroy him if you take him to a police station.'

George turned. 'Boyd, did you go out today?'

Boyd shrank back. Suzie stayed with him. 'Of course he didn't,' she retorted. 'He can't get out. That's a silly question to ask.'

'Let him answer for himself, Miss.'

Beth took a couple of steps forward. 'Hello Boyd. You remember me, don't you?'

Boyd nodded and relaxed his grip on Suzie.

'The Inspector's not going to hurt you, Boyd,' continued Beth gently. 'He just needs to find out a few things. The main one is, did you leave your room today?'

Boyd shook his head.

'Boyd,' James joined Beth, 'something rather ghastly has happened. I'm afraid that your auntie Jeannie is dead.'

The young man stepped back and sucked air in. He searched Suzie's eyes for confirmation.

'You can come and live with us now, Boyd,' she said. 'We'll make sure you're free.'

'Suzie,' Lucy admonished, 'don't make promises like that. You know we've no room.'

Suzie turned on her heels. 'Then we'll live here. There's plenty of room here.'

The two sisters entered into a debate. George joined James, Beth and the Merryweathers.

'What do you make of this Boyd chap? Truthfully.'

'I think he's innocent,' Anne stated.

'I-I've no idea,' said Stephen, 'b-but I do feel that he is the victim. S-surely someone would have seen him at the festival? He'd stick out like a bluebell in the snow.'

George switched his attention to Beth. 'I know you've got a soft spot for him but, emotions aside, what do you think?'

'I agree with Stephen. Jeannie wasn't a large woman but she was tough and that boy there is like a skeleton and fearful of her. I can't imagine him having the strength to strangle anything except a field mouse.'

'James?'

'I'm with the majority.' James smoothed his hair back. 'George, I think the girls are right. Boyd would be scared to death being hauled to a police cell. He can't even move from his own bedroom! Why not station a constable here on twenty-four-hour guard? His cousins could probably move in until something more stable comes along.'

'W-what a splendid idea,' said Stephen.

George pulled a face. 'What if the girls are guilty?'

James started. 'Goodness, I hadn't thought of that.'

He observed the girls as they debated their opinions. They'd more or less admitted to hating Christie and his sister. They'd attended the festival and had just announced to Boyd that he was now free to live with them. Was Locksmith Joe responsible, or did the girls plan this? Were he, Beth and the Merryweathers rooting for cold-blooded killers?

George reminded him that they'd be interviewing the girls later and announced that, provided everything was in order, James' idea was a good short-term solution. He called Lucy over to explain his decision. Lucy, although flustered, thought it was a good idea.

'We can move in here for a couple of nights. It's awkward for work, but we'll manage.'

'I'll need you down the station first,' said George. 'The pair of you.'

Beth suggested that she and Anne stay with Boyd until they returned. Lucy closed her eyes in thanks and made for the door.

Suzie skipped up to James and whispered in his ear. 'Can we meet tomorrow?'

'Of course. You have our telephone number.' He pulled her back. 'If you want my help, I must insist that you're honest with me at all times.'

She met his gaze and gave her promise.

13

That evening, James and Beth made their way through the bar of the Half Moon, stopping here and there to chat to villagers, farmers and shopkeepers. The festival was due to finish late afternoon, but had continued on into the evening. Children had been put to bed and those villagers who were able to, flocked to enjoy the hospitality of Donovan and Kate Delaney.

In the back room of the bar, Bob Tanner and the Taverners were leading a spontaneous 'come-all-ye', a folk music session where floor singers were welcome to perform. Someone struck up a chorus and the harmonies around the room sent tingles down James' spine. On the far end of the bar, Kate had laid out a number of cakes and pastries, left over from the WI tables. Tobacco smoke hung in the air.

'Ah, yer man, Lord Harrington,' said Donovan in his soft Irish lilt. 'Are you wanting the Autumn Gold now?' He took on a sarcastic expression. 'We've no tea, I'm afraid.'

James offered him a bashful smile and asked for a pint of Gold. Beth opted for a half of mild and a bag of peanuts.

Ducking under oak beams, they saw Bert commandeer a table and weaved their way to join him.

'Oi, oi,' he said. 'You joining me?'

'Unless you're expecting someone else, yes.'

Bert nudged two chairs out with his feet, pushed his cap back and began preparing a roll-up. 'Bit of a rum do, ain't it? All this business with that Cameron lot? You got yer feet under the table?'

'If you mean am I investigating,' said James, 'I may have a little sniff around, yes.'

Bert's face became a map of contours when he grinned. 'Thought as much. You got anything yet?'

'No,' said James, and then went through the details of the day. Beth added forgotten bits and pieces, including the extra scarecrow.

Bert let out a low whistle. 'Someone's done their 'omework, then?'

James frowned. 'Why?'

'Stands to reason, don't it? Who's gotta scarecrow outfit lying about?'

'Sweetie, he's right,' said Beth. She lowered her voice. 'This was premeditated, it must have been. Someone has prepared a scarecrow costume as a disguise.'

'Possibly, although it doesn't take a costume designer to dress up like a scarecrow,' replied James. 'Bert here is a fine example of that.'

Bert's eyes went heavenward as James grinned.

'But you may be right,' he continued. 'I do feel that someone persuaded her to come to the festival; a festival she'd refused to attend. And, within an hour of arriving, she's murdered.' He rapped the table. 'If that's the case, then the young lad's calculations were correct. There *were* twenty-six scarecrows.'

'I s'pose George is on the case?'

'You suppose correctly, my friend.'

Beth waved to Anne and Dorothy. 'I'm going to love you and leave you. I want to speak with Anne about GJ and Catherine.'

'Oh Lord.' He wagged a finger at her. 'Don't take over. Remember, this is *their* day.'

She grinned at James. 'I wouldn't dream of it.'

They watched as she threaded her way through the crowd. James cradled his pint jug and turned to Bert.

'You know, that man at the festival I saw — the one that appeared to shock Jeannie Cameron. I wondered whether it was that convict chap — whether he was the extra scarecrow?'

Bert spluttered over his pint. 'What, Locksmith Joe?'

'Yes. I've only seen a grainy black and white photograph, but he had the right build, a bushy beard and awful eyes.'

'What d'yer mean, awful eyes?'

'Difficult to explain, but quite unnerving.'

'Don't sound like Joe.'

James leaned in. 'I didn't think you knew him.'

Bert shifted in his seat and briskly denied any link. 'I know *of* him, that's all.

It don't sound like Locksmith. That's all I'm saying.'

'Well, there was menace in the eyes and I think Jeannie Cameron saw it too. If you don't know him, how can you comment?'

'Tch, what is this, the third degree?' replied Bert. 'I met him a couple o' times, at the races, that's all. And 'e didn't 'ave *awful* eyes.'

James settled back in his chair and studied his old friend, who had resumed drinking and was taking a keen interest in the darts match. He swirled the golden beer in his glass, more convinced than ever that Bert was holding back. He knew Locksmith Joe better than he was letting on. But what did he know? Was he shielding an escaped convict?

James crossed his legs. 'Why is he called Locksmith Joe? He's a killer, isn't he?'

Bert denied the accusation. 'He's done a few bits o' time here and there; all of 'em for robbery. That's how he got 'is nickname. Didn't always nick anything neither; sometimes he'd be asked to get inside an 'ouse and take photos of antiques and silver. He'd pass that on to dodgy dealers, who'd then do the job 'emselves so they knew they'd get the choice cuts, not the rubbish.' He leant across and placed his empty glass on the bar. 'Family man, is Joe. Two grown-up kids and a granddaughter.'

James was beginning to get an understanding of the man but noted the avoidance of the notion of murder. Although the chatter around the bar was lively, the silence between them became awkward. Bert pulled his chair closer.

'Word on the street is he's out to clear 'is name.'

James sat up.

'He's doing time for murder and he ain't a killer.' Bert lifted a finger as if to emphasise his point: 'That's the word on the street, not from me. But, when I met 'im, I didn't see a killer.'

'Why didn't he hang?'

Bert shrugged. 'Mitigating circumstances. And the courts aren't so keen on 'anging these days as they used to be.' He wiped his lips with the back of his hand. 'I'm off. I'll be in touch.'

James frowned over his friend's rapid departure, only to realise why when George Lane took his place. He pondered Bert's behaviour and attitude to the escaped convict and decided he was far more involved than he was letting on. The thought didn't sit right with him. Now he was sitting opposite another dear friend, a Detective Chief Inspector, who would have hauled Bert in straight away for questioning had he witnessed their earlier conversation.

'Everything all right, James?'

James broke from his thoughts and convinced his friend that everything was quite satisfactory. 'How did your chat with the nieces go?'

'Not much to say, really. They used to visit the Camerons a lot when the aunt was still alive. Sounds like this Auntie Gwen was quite normal compared to Christie and Jeannie. When she died, their visits became less frequent, although Suzie was always keen to see Boyd.'

'They seem close.'

'Not much difference in their ages and Suzie feels sorry for him. She used to visit

Boyd during the summer holidays and spent all her time with him.'

James studied his hands. 'Capable of murder?'

'Everyone's capable of murder, James, in the right circumstances. But I've nothing to hold them on. GJ was sure the girls were in the marquee when this was going on although he couldn't guarantee it. They've promised me that they're not going anywhere — they're stopping up at Cory House for the time being and I've got a constable posted there.'

'What about their parents?'

'Died in a road accident two years ago.'

'Oh Lord.'

'Lucy's a secretary in a typing pool and Suzie works in Woolworths. They just about make ends meet.'

'Any luck with finding Locksmith Joe?'

George took out his pipe. James watched as he filled the bowl and carefully lit the tobacco. Taking two or three quick puffs, he settled back with an air of contentment.

James grinned. 'You have something, don't you?'

George allowed himself a brief smile. 'I do and I don't, but it'll interest your enquiring brain.'

James brightened. 'Well, spit it out, man.'

'Locksmith Joe was jailed for the murder of Mrs Gwen Cameron, wife of Christie.'

'Good Lord. I mean . . . well, good Lord.' James stared at George. 'But does that help?'

'Of course it helps! It connects the escaped convict with the Camerons, but I don't know why he'd want to kill off the whole family. As far as I can make out from the reports, it was a robbery gone wrong. But he's more of a suspect than the girls or Boyd.' George took a puff. 'Our people have established that Christie had had a heavy dose of a sleeping draught and Jackson was right to question those marks on his neck — there seemed to be a mixture of strangulation and smothering.'

'So definitely murder,' said James. 'And, if he was doped up with sleeping powders, he was an easier target to kill.'

'Could be, although I'm keeping my

options open. Something doesn't sit right with me about this. Regardless of who killed Cameron Christie, how did they get into a room locked from the inside? The family have more access around the house. If Locksmith Joe was involved, surely he'd nab Christie outside — not chance it inside the house.' He checked his watch. 'Best get back to the station. Suzie Cameron let slip that she was seeing you tomorrow, is that right?'

'Yes, she rang earlier to arrange everything.'

'Let me know what she says.' He made his way out.

James picked up a beer mat and rotated it through his fingers. Bert was up to something with Locksmith Joe — had he got too involved? Locksmith Joe killed Christie's wife and had now escaped from prison. Why kill again if he was trying to clear his name. Bert refused to believe Joe was a killer and he felt he had to respect that. He'd always placed great trust in his friend's instinct and he wouldn't normally question that. But the evidence must have been there to put him in prison. The

Camerons moved from Yorkshire to Cavendish, the area where Locksmith Joe was hiding — was that a coincidence? Did Jeannie Cameron drug her brother and then kill him? It would certainly be easier to strangle someone if they were in a drug-induced sleep. Was she trying to set up Boyd? A boy unwanted by the family? Did Boyd find out and kill the aunt?

James snapped out of his thoughts when Beth plonked herself down in the chair opposite.

'Well, sweetie, we've some ideas to put to GJ and Catherine about decorating the church at Christmas for their wedding.'

He fell back into a daydream and only came out of it when Beth patted his hand. 'James?'

'Sorry, darling.'

He feigned innocence as Beth's beady-eyed stare met his. 'You're putting your Sherlock hat on.'

James said that he was and updated her about his discussion with George, finally adding that he would make a few enquiries. 'After all,' he added, 'people appear happy to divulge things to me that they wouldn't normally tell the police.'

Beth gave him a 'be careful' look. He held his hand up. 'I'll let George know if I find anything.'

14

The following morning, Elsie's café buzzed as customers from surrounding villages met for tea, pastries and gossip. James held the door open for Beth to enter, before undoing his overcoat. The delightful aroma of cinnamon-toasted teacakes and freshly baked scones greeted them. Most of the tables were full, but Beth had called ahead to ask if Elsie would mind holding a table. True to form, she'd placed a 'Reserved' sign on their favourite table by the bow window. They negotiated their way to it with a few 'hellos' to familiar faces en route.

Elsie appeared at the counter, a little flustered by the heat in the kitchen and the sudden influx of customers. She made a beeline for them.

'Hello, Lord Harrington, Lady Harrington. Lovely to see you.'

The door swung open and Suzie burst in with a smile. 'So sorry I'm late, the bus almost forgot to stop.' She joined them at the table, where James introduced her to Elsie.

'Suzie and her sister are going to be staying up at Cory House for a short while.'

'Ooh,' Elsie said in a whisper. 'That's where that fella died, isn't it? And weren't his sister . . . ' She brought a hand to her chest. 'You all right staying there?'

Suzie checked her hair in a compact mirror. 'It's cold and damp, but Uncle Christie had arranged workmen to come in over the next few months, so it'll be nice eventually. At least we'll have loads more room than at that awful place in Hove. And no rent to pay.'

'They're nieces to the Camerons,' Beth put in.

'Indirectly,' Suzie asserted. 'Our aunt married into the family.' She perused the menu and then mumbled. 'Must have been mad.'

James wiped the condensation on the window and stared out. 'Is Lucy not coming?'

'I told her to come later. She's always telling me to be quiet. Anyway, she has to come later because that stuffy Inspector called by to talk to Boyd.' She teased her hair. 'I can't see why he keeps pestering him. He hasn't done anything wrong.'

Elsie smiled at James and cleared her throat. 'We're still serving morning coffee and tea. We've also got hot buttered crumpets, toasted teacakes and a fresh batch of scones. But, if you like, I could cook something from the lunch menu.'

'No need for that, old thing. I think we're all fine with tea.'

'Not for me,' Suzie said. 'It's more modern to have coffee now. You know, in London they do that sort of thing all the time. I've been to the 2i's. I bet you've never been there.'

James repressed a grin. How old did this girl think he was? Just because he lived in the sticks didn't mean he was detached from modernity. The 2i's was *the* coffee bar to be seen in as a youngster in London, an extra draw being the number of skiffle groups and rock'n roll singers it featured. He corrected the order.

'Do your scones come with strawberry jam and cream?'

'Of course. Mrs Keates' home-made jam. She made up quite a bit during the summer and popped in with a few jars yesterday.'

James had met Mrs Keates the previous year, when she'd charmed him with her baking skills. They put an order in.

'It'll all be with you in five minutes.' Elsie went back to the kitchen.

James continued gazing through the window. 'Autumn is a beautiful season, don't you think?'

Beth agreed. Opposite them was ancient woodland that stretched the length of the road between Cavendish and Charnley. The mixture of trees presented a living tapestry of reds, golds, yellows and rusts. James felt contentment flow through him as he took the view in. All was right in the world when nature could blast your senses so spectacularly.

Suzie broke into his thoughts. 'Are we going to talk about trees or something interesting, like the reason I'm here?'

She shrank back from James' stern expression.

'I'm sorry, I didn't mean it to come out like that. It's just that I'm worried about Boyd.'

Elsie presented their refreshments.

147

There was a plate of scones with individual dishes of Mrs Keates' jam and Cornish clotted cream delivered, apparently, by a family friend who lived in Penzance.

Beth played mother and slid a cup of coffee across the table. 'What would you like to talk about, Suzie?'

'You don't think Boyd's going to be murdered, do you?' Suzie asked, her voice ringing out dramatically.

The people at the neighbouring table hushed. James smiled an apology and requested that Suzie keep her voice down. The young girl shrugged.

'I'm only being realistic. I couldn't bear the thought of something happening to him.'

'Why would someone want Boyd killed?' Suzie shrugged again.

'You spent quite a bit of time with him when he was younger,' said James. 'Is that true?'

Her eyes lit up. 'Oh, we had so much fun. I used to spend all of my school holidays with him. When Auntie Gwen was alive, she was so welcoming. She used to dress Boyd up from head to toe to protect his skin and give him sunglasses, too. He reminded me of a spy or someone undercover.' She laughed. 'We used to collect frogspawn and he'd keep it in a tank in his room. Auntie Gwen was such a wonderful mother.'

Beth stirred her tea. 'And when your auntie died?'

The young girl slumped. 'It was horrid. I'd still go up, but it wasn't because I was invited. But if I didn't go up, then Boyd had no one to play with and I wanted to make sure he got Calvin's letters. And we had to play inside.'

She gazed into her coffee cup as she described a large, bleak property on the outskirts of Otley and how, in time, Christie and Jeannie prevented Boyd from going outside at all. Tears welled up.

'It was as if they were ashamed of him. They called him a freak.'

Beth started. 'Oh, that can't be true. You wouldn't say that to your own child.'

'They didn't say it *to* him. They said it behind his back. I heard them once, when I was in the hall. They were talking about Boyd and his brother and didn't have a good word to say about either. Jeannie Cameron said that Auntie Gwen had cursed the family. I remember Uncle Christie talking to someone who belonged to his club in London and he had nothing good to say about Boyd.'

James' ears pricked. 'Club in London? I thought they lived in Yorkshire?'

'He used to visit London for his work and he went to a club there — the Wend something or other.'

'The Wendover?'

'Yes. Do you know it?'

'I'm a member myself, although I rarely frequent the place. D'you know the name of his friend? It's quite a select membership.'

Suzie racked her brains. 'Cheek? Chick? Chee . . . something like that.'

'Cheeseman? Could it be Cheeseman?'

She sat up with a start. 'Yes, yes, I think that's it. He called him something else, sometimes. Like a nickname.'

'Swiss?'

Suzie let out a gasp. 'Yes.'

Beth cried, 'You know him?'

'In passing. He loves Swiss cheese and,

of course, with a name like Cheeseman, the nickname rather suited him.' James turned his attentions back to Suzie. 'Is Boyd's brother an albino?'

Judging by Suzie's reaction and description, James decided that the brother must resemble a matinée idol. Calvin, he learnt, was tall, dark and handsome with deep brown eyes and a smile that would melt the North Pole. Beth said that she assumed Calvin was probably rather attractive to the opposite sex. Suzie beamed mischievously.

'They hovered like bees round a honey pot.'

'Goodness,' said Beth, 'I'm guessing that went against Mr Cameron's morals.'

'Calvin left home when he was fifteen. He pinched some money from Uncle Christie and got on a boat. Ended up in India.'

'Doing what?'

Suzie pulled an uninterested face and announced that she'd no idea. 'I haven't seen him for years and he never kept in touch with me. He still writes to Boyd, though.'

'So I understand,' said James. 'Listen, Suzie, why exactly are we here?'

The young girl chewed her lip and checked over her shoulder to the door. Was she waiting for Lucy, or hoping she wouldn't come? James couldn't be sure. She fiddled with her spoon.

'What's going to happen to Boyd?' she asked. 'Unless Calvin can get him back to India quickly, they'll put him in some sort of home. Anything we rent would be too small and we only just scrape by on what we earn. There's nothing wrong with him.'

Beth patted her hand. 'Suzie, I'm sure Boyd will be taken good care of. They don't put people into institutions unless they have good reason. Albino people are no different to us. All Boyd needs is some confidence and I think we know just the person who can help.'

'Really?'

James knew he must have looked confused. 'Who do we know that can help?'

'Oh James, you were only talking about him last night.'

'Of course, yes. Kushal Patel.'

Now it was Suzie's turn to be puzzled.

'Kushal Patel is an Indian chap who helped people during the war,' explained James. 'People who had faced adversity, violence, danger, that sort of thing. He sort of debriefed them, got their confidence back. I think this'll be right up his street.'

'So you'll help?'

'We can but ask, young lady, and I feel that this Patel chap would be delighted to help. I'll telephone him when we get home.'

Suzie quietly clapped. 'Oh, I do hope he can help. I loathed my aunt and uncle and I know it's quite awful what's happened. But don't you see how wonderful this would be for Boyd?'

James suggested that it was perhaps a little early to start celebrating and mildly chastised Suzie for even thinking it. But nothing could squash Suzie's excitement that Boyd would, at last, be his own man. As Beth engaged in small talk, he couldn't help but wonder if Suzie was, in some small way, responsible for the deaths of her aunt and uncle. She seemed ecstatic to be rid of them. Before he could ponder any further, though, the café door swung open and Lucy, holding her handbag, dashed to their table.

'Oh Lord Harrington, Lady Harrington.' She grabbed Suzie's hand as she took her seat. 'They've taken Boyd in for questioning.'

Suzie covered her mouth with her hands and Beth did her best to soothe her. James met Lucy's eyes.

'Have they arrested him?'

'No, but they found something.' She bit her lip. 'A scarecrow costume. Boyd was at the festival.'

Beth handed a tearful Suzie a handkerchief and grimaced at James. He had to think quick.

'Ladies, for want of a better suggestion, this is what I propose. Detective Chief Inspector Lane has a job to do and, bearing in mind the discovery of this costume, it's natural that he'll want to speak with Boyd. You girls get on to Mr Bateson in Cavendish. He's the local solicitor and I'm sure he won't mind going down.'

Lucy's shoulders dropped. 'But I can't afford a solicitor!'

James apologised for making such an assumption. 'All right. Well, I'll call George. He knows the situation with Boyd. He will make exceptions in the way he's handled. He's not completely unsympathetic.'

Suzie implored that James call Mr Patel.

'Who's Mr Patel?' said Lucy.

James held a finger up to silence everyone. 'Suzie will update you on our discussion. I will call Mr Patel. You girls return to Cory House and ensure that Boyd is looked after when he returns, as I am sure he will.'

Suzie blew her nose. 'But what if he doesn't return?'

'If he's not been arrested, George is going simply by the fact that Boyd was at the festival. That is not proof of murder. I say, Lucy, did George mention anything or do anything to make you think otherwise?'

Lucy shook her head, but had a somewhat guilty air about her. Beth also picked up on this.

'Are you keeping something back?' Beth asked.

Lucy said that the police had searched

Boyd's room. 'I don't know what they were looking for, but Boyd's letters were not in their normal place.'

'The letters from Calvin?'

'Yes. I told Boyd to keep them safe. He likes to read them now and again. He's hidden them, I'm sure, but I don't know where.' She paled. 'You don't think there's something incriminating in them, do you?'

James met her gaze. 'Would there be something he doesn't want the police to see?'

'Oh, goodness, it's all too upsetting for words.' She checked her watch. 'Come along, Suzie, the bus is due in a couple of minutes. You stay at the house; I have to get back to work.'

After a hasty goodbye, Suzie and Lucy tumbled out of the café and ran to the stop in time for the arriving bus. James called Elsie across and asked for some fresh tea. He turned to Beth.

'Well, darling, the game is afoot, as they say. Do you fancy a drive up to Richmond to meet Kushal Patel and an hour shopping while I call at the Wendover?'

'That sounds perfect.'

15

Beth contemplated the vista before her. 'Oh, how perfectly beautiful.'

The River Thames meandered through the valley below. James had parked the car at the top of Richmond Hill. The panorama beneath them would have been enjoyed by residents and visitors for several hundred years. Indeed, the main promenade was the subject of many paintings, writings and poems and Beth could understand why.

'Look at the trees,' she said. 'It reminds me of a Kashmir rug woven in gold and rust.'

A weak sun glinted on the autumn leaves; crows cawed and, in the distance, James could make out a family of swans gliding down the river past moored rowing boats. They heard the muted chug-chug of a wooden cruiser as it came into view. He breathed in the fresh air then checked his watch.

'Come along, darling. Mr Patel is just across the road here.'

They stood patiently at the front door as James pushed the ivory button for the bell. Shortly after, Kushal Patel, wearing a broad smile, swung the door open.

'Lord Harrington,' he said in a warm, Indian accent. 'It is most pleasing to see you again.' He reached out, grasped James' hand, then Beth's. 'And your beautiful wife, Lady Harrington.'

Beth tilted her head; her eyes danced at such a wonderful welcome. He chivvied them through to the front room where James had first set eyes upon Kushal a few months previously. It had been back in the spring, during his investigation into Delphine Brooks-Hunter that this gentle Indian came to his attention. James had warmed to him straight away and the compassion and kindness Kushal had shown Delphine only served to increase those sentiments.

Kushal Patel was a slim man in his seventies with smooth skin, liquid brown eyes and an easy smile. His long, slender fingers indicated the chairs by the window.

'You remember this room, Lord Harrington?'

'It would be difficult to forget it, Mr Patel. I certainly recall commenting on the view.'

'And I remember that we were too formal with our speaking. You must call me Kushal.'

James sat beside Beth and insisted that Kushal use their first names. Kushal rang a small hand-bell and a pretty Indian girl of around eighteen entered. She took an order for tea, smiled at James and Beth and disappeared. After a few minutes of small talk, she reappeared with a trolley and placed a solid silver teapot on the table alongside a matching sugar bowl and tea strainer. To one side was a dish of butterfly cakes with a generous filling of vanilla butter-cream. She distributed plates and napkins. Kushal thanked the girl and asked that they not be disturbed.

As he prepared tea, Kushal asked that James update him on any news since their last meeting. James and Beth did so and added any details he'd missed of the Brooks-Hunter affair before imparting the news of GJ's engagement. A smile spread across the Indian's face.

'That is wonderful news.' His eyes widened. 'Would it be permissible for me to attend the wedding?'

Beth's eyes glinted. 'GJ already has you on the list.'

'That is most delightful.' He gently brought the tips of his fingers together. 'And now I think it is time for you to tell me the reason for your visit.'

James went through the events to date: the arrival of the Camerons, their reluctance to socialise, their strict beliefs, the estranged elder son, the younger albino brother and his treatment. Beth added snippets of information here and there and Kushal reacted accordingly; a nod here, an 'oh dear' there, a catch of breath. They then described the discovery of Christie Cameron, the locked doors and the behaviour of the sister, Jeannie. This was followed by how the sister was now lying dead beside her brother in the morgue and an update on how the police were proceeding.

When they finished, James gave Kushal a 'that's it' gesture and silently hoped that this man might have some divine wisdom that could help. He watched as Kushal dropped one cube of sugar into his tea. He allowed it time to dissolve before stirring. All the time, James felt the Indian was turning the information over in his head, formulating an impression of the incident and the personalities involved. The mantel clock chimed a quarter past the hour. Kushal allowed some silence before responding.

'I know that you come to me in my professional capacity. You are worrying about the son, Boyd.'

James said he was. 'I wondered if you were able to spend some time with him, perhaps gain his confidence or, indeed, *give* him some confidence. The boy is frightened and the cousins are terrified he's going to be put away somewhere.' He took Beth's hand. 'Beth is really the only person whom I've seen gain his trust.'

Kushal reacted as if he knew that already. 'Your wife has a gentle energy, James. She has an aura about her, but . . . ' He turned to Beth. 'I believe that you feel unqualified, yes?'

Beth reached for her teacup. 'Most certainly, yes. After James described what you did for Delphine all those years ago . . . and for other war heroes, too. Well . . . I suggested he contact you.' Her eyes pleaded. 'Do you think you can help?'

Kushal beamed. 'I am most delighted to help.'

'We'll pay for your time,' James put in.

Kushal gave him a vigorous shake of the head. 'You will do no such thing. You were most ingenious with your investigations into Delphine's death. This is my thank you for those efforts that you put in.' He rang the bell and gave an affirmative nod of the head. 'I think that there must be no delay. If Boyd is in police custody, this is very, very frightening for him. You will allow me to travel back with you?'

James expressed his surprise and delight. 'Well, yes of course. I have one further engagement here. We can do that now and pick you up in, say, three hours. Is that suitable?'

The Indian girl reappeared.

'Prerna, I need an overnight bag.' Kushal turned to James. 'Do you have a place for me?'

Beth was delighted to invite him to stay.

'That is most satisfactory.' He returned his attentions to the girl. 'I will be away for two nights, possibly three.' He checked the clock on the mantelpiece. 'Yes, I will be ready in three hours.'

★   ★   ★

After dropping Beth off at Liberty's, James manoeuvred the car along two further streets and parked outside the Wendover. He took the steps two at a time and entered the serenity of the gentleman's club to be greeted by the doorman, Graves.

'Lord Harrington, welcome back, sir. We haven't seen you for several months.'

Graves helped him shrug his overcoat off and take his trilby and gloves.

'Not had the time, old chap. Always seem to have things to do.'

'Harrington's is securing an excellent reputation, your Lordship.'

James agreed and said that it was all coming along splendidly. He could always rely on Graves to know everything about the Wendover's members, regardless of how little they frequented the place. The man, dressed in grey tails and a top hat, was about the same age as James and seemed to be on duty whenever he came by, day or night. He wondered if the man ever slept.

After the usual pleasantries, he strode through to the lounge and was struck with a wall of tobacco smoke and the smell of old leather. A coal fire spat furiously in an inglenook fireplace. A good many elderly members were hidden from view, enveloped in large armchairs and engrossed in *The Times* or *Country Life*.

He lit a cigarette and wandered around the club. A man with a healthy complexion made a double take.

'James?'

James knew he must have looked delighted, partly through seeing his old acquaintance again, but mostly in relief that the man he wanted was here. 'Swiss, how are you?'

Andrew 'Swiss' Cheeseman stood the same height as James and was dressed in a smart black suit with a faint pinstripe.

His shoes were clean enough to eat off and his manicured fingers curled the ends of his moustache. James accepted the offer of a brandy. They ensconced themselves in antique leather chairs in the far corner of the oak-panelled room.

'So, James, what the devil are you doing here? You're rarely in town and, when you are, it's not to visit the Wendover. How's your wife?'

'She's very well. Thank you for asking. To be honest, although I'm rarely in town these days I'm loath to let the membership slip, especially as this was my father's favoured watering hole. I came up to see you, actually.'

Swiss raised a questioning eyebrow.

'You knew Christie Cameron, is that right?'

Swiss grimaced and indicated that he wasn't someone he'd go out of his way to socialise with.

'Oh, why's that?'

'You've met him?'

'I have.'

'Would *you* want to socialise with him?'

James accepted this as a fair argument.

'Well, aside from his social skills, did you know much about him?'

Swiss shrugged. 'Lived in Glasgow for a time. I think that's where he was from originally. But then he moved to Yorkshire. I believe he lives with his sister. His wife was killed a few years ago. Has two sons.'

'Did he speak much about his wife?'

Swiss shrugged. 'He never really spoke much about her or what happened to her, but I got the impression there was something odd. I remember asking what happened, more out of compassion than anything, but he cut me short. Said he didn't want to talk about it, which I thought was fair enough. Grief hits people in different ways.'

'And his sons?'

'I met the older one once. He came to London with Christie to see the sights. Must have been about eleven or twelve. Nice young man, polite; I heard he set up a company in India.' He frowned. 'Went into business with a friend . . . Joe, Josh, something like that. Funny what you remember, isn't it?'

'Something in particular?'

'I always remember the boy going on about what he and the younger brother got up to and Christie demanded he stop referring to him.'

'Referring to the younger brother?'

'Yes. I got the impression he was a bit backward or something; as if something wasn't quite right about him. He was given an education at home, whereas the older brother attended a school. That's a bit odd, isn't it?' Swiss swirled the brandy in his glass. 'Why do you need to know, anyway?'

'Christie Cameron died a few days ago.'

'Ruddy hell,' said Swiss, sitting up in his chair. 'How do you know?'

'He moved to Cavendish a few weeks ago. Now both he and the sister have been murdered.'

Swiss stared at him, open-mouthed. 'Crikey. Cavendish? What did he move to Cavendish for?'

James was clueless and said he was hoping Swiss would have some insight into that. Swiss declared that he didn't.

'I didn't know him well. I used to steer clear of him, if I could. Always ranting on about sin and morals. I mean, I'm a churchgoer, James; I go along on a Sunday and all, but he was strict, strict Presbyterian.'

They sat in thoughtful silence for a while.

'How did you get to know him?' asked James at last.

'Work. He owned a steel works in Glasgow and then opened up a factory in Yorkshire and moved there. He used to invest in stocks and shares and always liked to meet the people he invested with.'

'That's where you came in?'

Swiss nodded. 'My company looked after a few of his investments. I didn't deal with him directly, that fell to my colleague, Quinn.' He let out a *tut*. 'I suppose the sons will be in line for a windfall, then?'

'Windfall?'

'God, yes. The man was rolling in it. Never spent anything unless he had to. Must have a quarter of a million in stocks and shares through us alone. Those two sons are set up for life, and those girls too.'

James recoiled. 'What girls?'

'There were two cousins, lived on the coast. I remember the last time he had any dealings with us, he'd indicated that he should perhaps include them in his will. Part of his wife's family I believe.'

James raised an eyebrow. 'Now that is interesting.'

Swiss checked his watch and pushed himself up. 'Sorry, James, but this is lunch hour and I have an appointment back at the office. You can walk back with me if you like?'

James followed him through to the front desk. 'No can do. I've to pick Beth up at Liberty's and then head over to Richmond.' He held a hand out. 'Good to see you, Swiss. Mustn't leave it so long next time.'

'Always here,' he replied and handed James a business card. 'But next time, telephone ahead and we'll lunch — bring your wife, too.'

James thanked Graves for the safe-keeping of his overcoat and hat. In forty minutes he and Beth were back in Richmond. He opened the boot of the car and placed Kushal's suitcase inside. On closing it, he held Kushal's arm.

'I say, if I wanted to know if someone was still living in India, would you have the contacts to establish whether or not they were?'

'Most certainly. Give me the details later and I will begin my enquiries.' He grinned. 'This reminds me very much of the spring, with you and this investigation business.'

In the car, Beth sat in the rear with Kushal and the pair of them chatted as if they'd known each other for years. When they arrived home, Beth insisted on giving Kushal a tour of the house and where he would be sleeping. Shortly after, the Indian declined the offer of tea and, instead, requested he be taken straight to the police station.

'That is why I am here, so that is where I should be.'

★ ★ ★

Kushal had been gone for a couple of hours when James began preparing the fire in the lounge. He stacked up some wood and newspaper and piled some coal on from the scuttle. A sound stopped him. Was that a knock on the back door? He made his way into the kitchen and opened the side entrance. A cool breeze greeted him and nothing more. He was about to close it when something caught his eye. On the step was a small box wrapped in brown paper. Curiosity drove him outside where he scrutinised the front of the house and the drive leading to the main road. Whoever left it had disappeared faster than a greyhound from a trap.

He picked the package up and frowned. The writing on the paper was neat and considered. James turned the parcel over for clues but found nothing to indicate where this had come from or who had delivered it. Returning to the kitchen, he closed the door and wandered, deep in thought, through to the hall.

Beth came down the stairs, fastening an

earring. 'What's that, sweetie?'

'I've no idea. Someone left it by the door leading to the kitchen.' He pulled the string: the paper fell away to reveal a shoebox. He slipped the lid off to disclose a pile of letters. Beth pulled one out.

'This is from India.' She shuffled through half a dozen. 'These are Calvin's letters to Boyd.' Her brow knitted. 'Who sent them? Boyd?'

James shrugged. 'I haven't a clue. If it was, why not knock on the front door and hand them to me?' A slip of paper fell to the floor. He picked it up. 'It isn't signed. It asks that we keep the letters safe.'

James replaced the lid.

'Do you think you're supposed to read them?' asked Beth.

'It doesn't invite me to do so. And they're private. It doesn't seem right to read them.'

'If they're private, why not bury them in the garden? Why leave them here?'

James suggested they make tea and chat with Kushal about it. 'I value his thought process. He always seems to do the right thing. And I also forgot to mention something. A nice surprise for us.'

He went on to explain that, when they were driving to the police station, Kushal had insisted that he make a traditional curry for them the following day.

'But I don't have any spices!' Beth said.

'He brought some with him.'

'Oh, how wonderful.'

James went through to the lounge and silently pondered the day. Cameron, he discovered, had been sitting on a fortune. Had George found his last will and testament? How much was the old man really worth? If Swiss was right with his valuation, there had certainly been motive for murder. But why leave a fortune to two sons he couldn't tolerate? And were the girls involved? The thought of Lucy and Suzie committing murder sent a shiver through him.

He studied the shoebox. Who had left it? Was he supposed to read the letters? Was Boyd as innocent as they all thought? Was there something in the letters that would incriminate him? If he had means to attend the festival, he must have had a key to his bedroom door. And if that was the case, did he also have access to his father's room?

James sighed. 'And where on earth does that leave Locksmith Joe?' he mumbled to himself.

16

On rising the next day, they found Kushal Patel had disappeared.

'His clothes are still here,' Beth said as she prepared the table for breakfast.

'Perhaps he goes for an early morning stroll. I'm going to give George a call and see how young Boyd is. I'm surprised he kept him at the station.'

On the occasional table by the front door, he found an envelope addressed to them which he opened.

He called out to Beth. 'There's a note from Kushal on the table. He's with George at the police station.'

'Goodness, he doesn't let the grass grow under his feet, does he?'

James picked up the receiver. 'Are we having soft-boiled eggs?'

'We are. I'm just waiting for the baker to arrive with fresh bread.'

As if on cue, the doorbell rang and the said baker stood there with a wide smile and a wicker basket full of loaves, rolls, crumpets and teacakes. As Beth made her order, James waited to be connected to George.

'Ah George, I understand you have Kushal with you.'

'Yes. He stayed until the boy went to sleep last night and was down here first thing. I must admit I wasn't sure about it, but he seems to be getting on well with the lad. He's certainly more comfortable than he was, although he still resembles someone with a gun pointing at his head.'

'And what's your thinking?'

He heard the flick of a match and gathered that George was lighting his pipe. 'I'm going to release him. He was at the scarecrow festival but claims he just wanted to go. I think Beth gave him such a wonderful description of it, he sneaked out and saw it for himself.'

'How did he get out?'

'Claims that Jeannie Cameron left the door unlocked.'

James commented that it wasn't like George to take his only suspect at his word. George cleared his throat.

'I just can't see the lad being involved in this. No, Locksmith Joe is my main suspect. There's another thing, too. Our doctor examined the body and reckons Jeannie Cameron was strangled by someone bigger than Boyd.'

'How so?'

'Marks around the neck. Boyd's not big, is he? I mean, he's only a boy. His hands are pretty small and he hasn't much strength.'

'Oh, I see. Indeed. I say, I heard something yesterday that may be of interest to you.'

James spent the next five minutes going over his meeting with Swiss at the Wendover. He highlighted what appeared to have been a split in the Cameron family and the apparent wealth of Christie Cameron.

An exasperated curse came down the line. 'James, how do you do it?'

'What?'

'You're always one step ahead of me. I suppose you're going to ask me about Cameron's will?'

'Well, if you're volunteering?'

'You're right. The old man was rolling in it.'

With some persuasion, George verified that Boyd and Calvin would benefit, along with Suzie and Lucy.

James let out a silent 'phew'. 'I don't understand why he would leave a fortune to two sons he had no time for.'

'Me neither.'

'You say you're releasing Boyd?'

'At the moment. He's to stay in Cavendish. We're taking him home later and we'll drop off Mr Patel at the same time.'

'Jolly good.' James was about to hang up when George stopped him.

'Have you seen much of Bert lately?'

Alarm streaked through James. 'Not as much as I normally do, no. Why do you ask?'

After some hesitation, George answered. 'I found out that Locksmith was hauled in several years ago about a robbery and Bert's name cropped up. Nothing proven; nothing ever is with Bert. I just wondered if he'd mentioned anything.'

James told him he hadn't and, putting

the receiver down, gave serious consideration to his old friend. What on earth was Bert playing at?

Beth popped her head out. 'Eggs ready in three.'

'Splendid.'

Following her into the kitchen he updated her about Boyd. She closed her eyes in relief.

'Oh, thank goodness. I couldn't bear the thought of him being locked in a cell any longer. I'm so pleased Kushal was there. I'm sure he was a tremendous help.'

James edged open the door leading to the gardens. The sky was battleship grey and the tops of the trees swayed in the wind. The early morning frost had turned to damp.

'These letters of Boyd's are enticing me. I have no idea whether I should or not, but I rather fancy taking a gander. What do you think?'

Beth spooned the eggs into their eggcups, buttered some toast and cut it lengthways into soldiers. 'I know what you mean. But, yes, I feel the same way.

Let's go through them with Kushal.' She looked past James to the gardens. 'It's not going to be much fun out there today. They're forecasting wind and showers this afternoon.' She handed him his plate of eggs and toast. 'And we have the theatre tonight.'

'Oh yes, I've been looking forward to that.'

Several weeks ago, James had rung his cousin, Herbie Harrington, who knew 'people' in the theatre world and managed to secure four sought-after tickets to see *The Mousetrap*. The Merryweathers were coming with them.

In the dining room, James turned on the wireless and tuned it to the Light Programme. Bing Crosby crooned 'Zing-a-little-Zong'.

Beth cracked the shell of her egg and pointed her spoon at him. 'Do you think it was Locksmith Joe who killed the Camerons?'

'I do,' he said and added that the police believed all roads led to Locksmith. He'd opted not to tell Beth of George's suspicions concerning Bert having been mentioned in connection with a robbery involving the convict.

'They can't see who else it could be, but I find it odd that he would risk killing Christie at home. Why not wait until he goes out? It must have been him at the scarecrow festival I saw. He certainly had the appearance of a man ready to throttle someone and he had the same build as in the description in the paper.' James dunked a toasted soldier into the soft yolk. 'But something doesn't sit right. I'm sure George isn't as convinced as he says he is.'

'So are you still going to read those letters?'

'Yes, but I won't let on to anyone that we've done so. I feel as if I am betraying a confidence.'

* * *

Later that afternoon, the three of them gathered in the kitchen and followed Kushal's instruction for cooking chicken curry. James was given the job of measuring out the spices, while Beth prepared the chicken, onions and mushrooms. Their friend heated fat in a large pan and added the spices and onions. The aromas of cumin, turmeric and chilli permeated the kitchen. He instructed Beth to boil water for rice, added the final ingredients to the pan and stirred in a chicken stock. Beth breathed in the spices.

'Mmm, Kushal, this smells divine.'

James followed suit. 'I say, can we have a taste?'

Kushal handed him a spoon. 'I hope it is not too spicy for you.'

James took a spoonful and closed his eyes. 'Goodness, that really is delicious. I wonder if we could nab the recipe from you?'

'I am pleased to share it with you. I will write the recipe for you before I leave.'

After lunch, Beth and Kushal perched on the edge of their seats waiting, in anticipation, for James to lift the lid off the shoebox. James hesitated and sought the approval of both Beth and Kushal. 'Are you sure we're doing the right thing, reading these?'

'Why else would they have been left?' asked Beth.

Kushal gave him a reassuring smile. 'The owner of these documents knew that he or she ran the risk of them being read. We are not giving a public speech. The contents will remain between the three of us.'

He lifted the lid.

In all, there were around forty letters bunched inside with varying degrees of wear. It was clear that some had been read more often than others. The envelopes were coloured grey with a blue 'Air Mail' logo printed on them. James took a deep breath and opened the envelope with the earliest stamp. Beth and Kushal looked on as James carefully unfolded the flimsy paper and immediately commented on the handwriting and how neat it was.

'Right, here we go:

Dear Boyd,
I have finally arrived in Bombay! Boyd, sailing is the most wonderful thing but, after so many weeks at sea, my legs feel like warm jelly and the world still moves when I stand still. It's like those men you see stumbling out of

pubs having had one whisky too many, although you probably don't remember that. You were too young. But, I'm finding my feet now and beginning to explore the area.

I have a couple of rooms close to the Victoria railway terminal and I'm a short walk away from the Gateway of India. I've enclosed a photograph of it which includes information on the back for you to read.

Our ship was full of elegant men and women who dispersed across the city as soon as we'd docked. I can only describe the city as vibrant and chaotic. The Indian people bend over backwards to be helpful and they smile a lot. I don't know why because most are exceptionally poor. But how I am going to get over this heat, I don't know. I'm more used to snow. It is devilishly hot, like a furnace.

Yesterday, I went to a market and have never seen anything like it. All my senses were assaulted by colours, spices, oils, silks and constant chatter. There was also an incessant ringing of bicycle bells and the occasional lorry blasting its horn. I also saw a cow wander across the road! Oh Boyd, how I wish you were here to see it.

Today, I am looking for work. Joshua's cousin has a contact here and I pray with all my heart that some employment will turn up. I will make enough, one day, for you to join me and experience this wonderful city at first hand.

I have written separately to Father. I fear that we will never see eye to eye. Until I am able to prove myself, I will not write to him again. All of my letters to you will go to Lucy as I am quite convinced Father will not pass them to you.

My dear brother, I will write often and ask that you forgive me for leaving you at such a young age. Please, do not forget me.

Calvin'

James replaced the letter and sought a reaction from Beth and Kushal. Kushal beamed.

'He is most accurate with his description of Bombay. The architecture around Victoria station is wonderful. It brought back many memories for me. I am wondering why he chose India to live?'

'Perhaps because of this contact of his,' said James.

'And who is this man Joshua?' asked Beth.

'Ah yes,' said Kushal, 'Josh is Calvin's school friend. Boyd mentioned him when we spoke. He remembered them being very close and grew up together.'

'Yes, Swiss mentioned him up at the club,' added James.

Beth chuckled to herself. 'Fancy seeing a cow crossing the road in the middle of a city.'

The Indian smiled. 'It is most common to see cows and goats, but occasionally there is an elephant. They are brought down from the hills when the ships arrive.'

'An easy way to make a profit from the tourist,' James suggested; Kushal agreed.

Beth took out the next letter and announced that it was dated six months later.

'Dear Boyd,

I am well and truly settled in my way of life here in Bombay. Yorkshire seems a million miles away and I believe the only thing I miss is you.

Employment here is good. Josh's cousin was able to provide an opening for me in shipping and I work for a cargo company, so much of my time is spent down at the docks. My office faces the Arabian Sea. I believe the Arabian Sea is as exotic as its name. Every day there are flotillas setting off from the quay; fishing boats, pleasure cruises and the huge ocean liners that have travelled hundreds of miles. My window is open wide to allow what little breeze there is to come in.

One exciting piece of news — Josh came to visit and decided to stay! He has managed to get employment with the same company. Having my school chum here is like old times and we have discovered a wonderful jazz club that serves New York-style martinis. I have enclosed some photographs of the pair of us outside the club. I know we *all look a mess The third person is Josh's cousin, Alastair.'*

Beth handed James a handful of small black and white photographs of three young men, all with dark hair and open-necked shirts. They flicked through them. They stood quite some distance from the camera and were raising their beers to whoever was taking the photograph. Their smiles were wide and the expressions on their faces radiated youth, vitality and freedom. Beth continued reading:

'I so wish I had the funds to rescue you from the clutches of Father. I can't believe he won't allow you outside. Good God, you are no different to me, Boyd. I cannot understand him. How can he believe that he is acting in a Christian way? Since Mother died, he appears to have become mad. Keep in touch with Lucy and Suzie and ask that they visit you often. I know it is difficult with them being so far away, but encourage Suzie to spend her days

with you. She mustn't allow the atmosphere in that house to dampen her spirit.

I have met a girl, Jayne. She's very nice and works as a secretary here in the company.

I've enclosed some Indian sweets for you. I hope you like them.

Study hard, baby brother, there is a life waiting for you here. Once I have the funds, I will come for you.

Calvin'

'Oh dear,' Beth said as she replaced the envelope. 'Isn't it terribly sad that Christie Cameron locked his son up like that?'

Kushal agreed with Calvin's questioning of Christie's faith. His eyes were earnest. 'Boyd is a thoughtful and articulate young man. I am sure that he will suffer the same discrimination with his paleness as those of us with dark skin.'

'Mmm,' said James, 'I hate to say it, Kushal, but I believe you're right. The vast majority of us rarely see beneath the surface. I confess I was one of those people in my younger days. My father was quick to expel that from me.'

After a moment of contemplation, Beth went through what they had so far. 'Calvin is in gainful employment and loving Bombay. He's desperate for Boyd to join him and Josh has emigrated.'

They each took letters, examined them and read snippets out here and there. Calvin continued to describe the sights and sounds of Bombay, the bars and clubs he visited with Josh and mentioned, in passing, the lady he'd been courting. Although they must only have been around seventeen or eighteen, Calvin and Josh had grown up fast. Boyd presumably loved the Indian sweets his brother had sent as he continued to receive boxes of sweets, along with clothing. James hushed everyone.

'Listen to this. This is two years ago:

Josh and me are starting our own business. This city is on the rise and people are flocking here. Although Father would never believe me, I did manage to learn quite a bit about building a business in my few years at home. Josh left the cargo business and has been working as a builder on land several miles north of here. He's seen many opportunities for a more professional building company. We launch the company in June. You will also have seen that I've mentioned a lady friend. Well, we are engaged to be married. I believe this may build bridges with Father. I have written to him to tell him my good news. Perhaps this will lighten his mood toward the world and you in particular.'

Kushal rested his elbows on the armchair and brought his fingers to a steeple.

'It is my belief that Calvin was perhaps the disappointment in the family. I think you refer to this being as the black sheep.' He sat forward. 'Many of his letters are most entertaining and he and Josh are visiting many clubs and bars. I wonder if womanising is behind the family split?'

Beth put her hand to her mouth. 'Oh goodness, you don't think he got a girl into trouble, do you?'

The Indian pulled a face and said that the idea wasn't out of the question.

'That makes perfect sense,' said James. 'He gets a girl into trouble. She's either gone ahead and had the baby or, God forbid, made the decision to visit one of those dreadful backstreet doctors you hear about. Either way, Christie Cameron would disown his son for that behaviour.'

'Oh, how awful,' said Beth.

'Calvin indicated in an earlier letter that he had to prove himself to make amends. Perhaps this is it. Perhaps getting married, settling down and starting a business would bring his father round.'

Kushal agreed. 'You are correct. Your detective friend let slip that Christie had changed his will recently. Calvin now benefits, whereas he did not before.'

James reached in for the next letter and held the envelope up. 'Oh I say, this one is typed.' He unfolded the letter to reveal type that had, in places, created tiny holes in the flimsy paper:

Dear Boyd
I have a typewriter! It's in our office

here in Bombay and I am trying to get to grips with it. I type with my two index fingers and it seems very time-consuming, but the more practice I have, the better.

Business was slow but is now on the up. I stay mainly in the office and get orders and do the paperwork. Josh is out on site making sure everything is being done properly. I haven't seen him for about two weeks as it's easier for him to stay there than keep coming back to the city. But we finished working on a block of accommodation last week and that's given us some more contracts. I'm putting money by every month now. I do not want you to travel by boat. The journey is long and arduous and you would be unhappy and lonely. Air travel is the way forward, so I propose flying back to England to get you. I have enough for my return flight. I just need to save enough for your ticket. I think I will have enough funds soon.

My other expense is Jane. I enclose a picture of her at our wedding. She's lived in India all her life. Her father was in the army and her mother was a seamstress. They're both dead now. I was most surprised to receive a short note from Father congratulating me. I felt no warmth from his words, but he would not have written this if my news had not touched him in some way. I wonder what sort of reception I will have when I eventually knock on his door. It's surprising what we do for love, isn't it?

Why is Father thinking of moving? He knows no one in the south of England, only a couple of men at the Wendover. What is he thinking? Has something happened? You mentioned Cavendish in your letter. I looked at an atlas and see that it is a tiny village in Sussex. But perhaps moving would be good. At least you will be closer to Lucy and Suzie. There are too many bad memories in that old house. Don't let it unsettle you, Boyd. I will get you over here. I cannot wait any longer and I don't care whether it puts me in debt.

I've enclosed a headband that many

young Indian men wear. Best not let Father see you in it, he would probably think it beneath you.

Take care of yourself, little brother. I will be in touch about flights.

Calvin'

'Well, that was written six months ago,' said James.

'Interesting,' mumbled Kushal.

James remained silent and waited for him to continue.

'I am thinking thoughts that I should not be thinking.'

'Well, whatever you say, Kushal, will remain between the three of us,' said James.

'These letters are showing an almost desperate need to have Boyd in India. I am wondering if he is already here?'

James raised an eyebrow. 'You mean something's changed in his circumstances?'

Kushal remained silent.

'Perhaps,' said Beth, 'he's not doing as well as he says in his letters. The last couple seem to be full of how successful he is.'

Kushal congratulated her on that insight. 'Often people will exaggerate the positives when the exact opposite is occurring.'

'And killed the father to get the inheritance?' replied James. 'How would he know he's a beneficiary? If the will was changed recently, would he know? But that does appear to coincide with Calvin wanting to get Boyd across to India.'

'Perhaps Christie mentioned the will in his congratulatory letter.'

The telephone rang. James walked over to the desk and picked up the receiver. He then waved it at Kushal, who leapt up and took it from him.

'Hello? Yes.' He appeared deep in thought. 'Thank you very much. You are most helpful.' He replaced the receiver. 'As far as the authorities can tell, Calvin Cameron had not left India at the time of his father's death. But, he has now left Bombay by aircraft and should be in the country now, depending on the route he has taken.'

Kushal stacked the letters in the shoebox and replaced the lid. Beth began tidying up.

She gave James a 'chin up' smile. 'Let's put this behind us for this evening. We have the theatre to attend.' She sat on the sofa by Kushal. 'Will you be all right on your own tonight?'

Kushal's eyes lit up. 'I do not own a television and I see that 77 *Sunset Strip* is on this evening. Many people I know speak of this programme. Am I able to watch it?'

James grinned and promised Kushal that he would, most certainly, be able to watch it. As Beth tidied away, James explained how to switch the television on and which buttons to use for the channels and volume. He'd liked to have watched it himself as it was proving to be an entertaining private detective series. But he had *The Mousetrap* to see that evening and a mystery of his own to solve here in Cavendish. Perhaps Agatha Christie would provide some inspiration.

★   ★   ★

Crowds spilled out of the theatres and onto the streets of London. As people passed one another, snippets of conversations could be heard about plays they'd seen, films enjoyed and restaurants either visited or yet to drop into. The evening was dry, but chilly, and a number of couples huddled outside bustling pubs, watching the traffic. Black cabs buzzed alongside red double-decker buses and bicycles weaved between them. A policeman, wearing his traffic band, took control of the queues building up along Shaftesbury Avenue.

James steered his group to The Salisbury in Covent Garden. It was a lively pub that his father had frequented because of his wartime friendship with the landlord. Built at the end of the nineteenth century, it was a triumph of gleaming mahogany, etched glass, bronzed nymphs and art nouveau light fittings.

He caught the landlord's eye then nudged Beth and the Merryweathers in the direction of the far window, where they found a small round table and four stools.

The landlord lifted the bar shelf and, throwing a tea towel over his shoulder, greeted them both. 'Lovely to see yer, your Lordship.' He bowed to Beth. 'Lady Harrington and guests. Haven't seen you in an age.'

'Rarely come up these days,' said James. 'How's your father?'

The landlord winced. 'Died last year. Heart attack we think, but his body was tired. I think he was ready to go.'

James expressed his condolences. Their respective fathers had both served in the Great War and an unlikely friendship had been forged between the two of them. Much like his friendship with Bert; some people were able to cross the classes and mix easily. The landlord leant on the bar.

'What can I get yer?'

'Two gin and tonics and two whisky and gingers.'

'Coming right up.'

'D-did you say B-Bert was joining us?' said Stephen.

'Yes,' said James. 'I believe he has more dress-material for the ladies.'

'That'll be for the wedding.' Anne clasped her hands together and beamed at Beth. 'I do so love a wedding.'

As the drinks arrived, Stephen told

James that Dorothy Forbes had joined the sewing group for the bridesmaid dresses and that Rose and Lilac Crumb were tasked with decorating the church. Although the December wedding was a couple of months away, James complimented everyone on their organisation and particularly picked out Stephen for his delegation skills.

'You certainly seem to know how to handle those Snoop Sisters, Stephen. I think you're the first to have been able to integrate them into the community.'

'M-many a lost sheep s-simply needs to feel loved.'

'Oi, oi,' came Bert's familiar greeting. He called out for a pint of IPA and dragged a stool across. 'And 'ow was *The Mousetrap*?'

'Wonderful,' said Beth, 'although none of us guessed the end and the cast have sworn us all to secrecy.'

Bert pushed his cap back. 'That's why Agatha's the best.' He pushed a large package across to James. 'Material.'

James secured it between him and Beth. 'How much do we owe you?'

'Nothin' Jimmy boy. Call it a wedding

present for GJ and Cath.'

'But what about travel expenses?'

'What travel expenses?'

They all laughed and James had to chuckle with them. Bert had the uncanny knack of getting something for nothing, or was able to barter and provide a service in return. He wondered if Bert ever paid full price for anything. He thought probably not.

'So, 'ow's the investigation going?'

'Slowly,' said James. 'George took young Boyd in for questioning and — '

'Boyd! He wouldn't 'urt a fly, would he? Can't 'ave him locked up.'

James leant toward him. 'How do you know?'

Bert's eyes shifted left to right. 'Just what I've 'eard, that's all. And Beth told me about 'im when she met 'im. That's not yer fella.'

Anne and Beth thanked him for the material and told them what they could about the play. James studied Bert. His behaviour over the last few days had been decidedly shifty. And what was this confidence about Boyd, a boy he'd never set eyes on? He took advantage of a break in the conversation.

'How do you know Boyd is not the chap? Do you know something?'

'Leave it,' replied Bert. 'Don't ge' involved in this one.'

'Is this something to do with Locksmith Joe?'

Bert forced a smile. 'Locksmith Joe? Of course not, wha' makes you think that?'

'He's dangerous, he's in the area and I'm sure he was at the festival when Jeannie Cameron died. He's a killer, Bert.'

Bert gritted his teeth. 'He didn't kill anyone. Locksmith Joe's a robber, that's all. A good one, too. He'd nick the salt off your chips if 'e could.' He eyeballed James. 'He ain't a killer.'

James whispered in his ear, 'I know your name cropped up in a robbery that he was involved in.'

Bert met his gaze for a second, gulped down the rest of his beer, said a curt goodbye and left the pub.

Beth looked on in horror. 'Sweetie, what on earth did you say to him?'

James swigged his whisky as he

watched his friend disappear into the crowds. 'I'm rather concerned that Bert may be into something he'll regret. He's always confided in me and he hasn't this time. Instead, I appear to have annoyed him.'

'He's e-either annoyed, James, or h-he's fearful,' said Stephen.

'Of what?'

'That you are too involved.'

'That's right,' said Anne. 'What did he say? Something like 'leave it alone'.'

'I know exactly what he said,' Beth put in. 'He said don't get involved in this one.'

James slowly rotated his glass on the table. There was no choice. He would have to tackle Bert and the sooner the better. He didn't want to think of his friend as being involved with this convict chap. And if Locksmith Joe was a killer, why was he so intent on wiping out the Camerons?

17

The following day James, accompanied by Charlie Hawkins, rang the doorbell at Cory House.

'My kids wanted to come today,' said Charlie, rolling his eyes. 'To see the ghost.'

James laughed. 'I take it they've never seen an albino before.'

'No, they haven't and neither have I, truth be told. But I know what'd happen if they came. They'd just stand and stare at him, poor tyke. They saw your Mr Patel in the village earlier and stood gawping.'

A young police constable answered the door and, recognising them, swung it open to allow them into the front room where Boyd was completing a jigsaw of the Houses of Parliament. His long-sleeved shirt was loose on his shoulders. His face lit up on seeing James, but wariness appeared when he spotted Charlie.

'Don't be alarmed, Boyd. This is a good friend of ours, Charlie Hawkins. He's the local librarian and he's brought you something.'

'Hello Boyd,' said Charlie. He stood his briefcase on a spare armchair, flipped it open and brought out two large books. He handed them to Boyd. 'James tells me that you have a brother in Bombay. Well, these are some picture books I found in the library. I've enrolled you so you've got them for three weeks. I've to have them back by the date stamped at the front of the book.'

Boyd held the books as if they were antiques and took the library membership card from him. His index finger stroked the name written on it — Boyd Cameron. Charlie sat down opposite Boyd and went through membership of the library, its opening hours and where he could find it.

'I live next door to the library,' said Charlie. 'If you want to visit when it's not open, knock on my door and I'll take you through.'

'Thank you,' Boyd whispered. He turned his attention to the books and opened the cover of the first one to reveal a large, colourful photograph of the Gateway of India. His eyes shone.

Charlie stood up and told James that he'd have to be going. 'I've left the library shut and it should be open. Just wanted to meet the lad myself.'

There came a sharp rap at the door. James found himself at the front door before the constable and went ahead and opened it. A young man with a deeply suntanned complexion, dark hair and an open, honest face smiled broadly. He held a large suitcase.

'Ah, hello. Is this the right place?'

'The right place being?'

'Cory House.'

Charlie said goodbye as James confirmed that this was, indeed, Cory House. He tilted his head. He couldn't place the accent; it seemed to be a mixture of all sorts.

The young man stretched out a hand. 'I'm Calvin. Calvin Cameron.'

James did a double-take, then grasped Calvin's hand warmly. 'Good Lord.' He shouted through to the front room.

'Boyd, your brother's here. Calvin.'

He noticed a nervousness about Calvin. Perhaps, with so many years having passed, he was fearful that his baby brother would be unenthusiastic about his arrival. Perhaps he thought Boyd wouldn't recognise him. After all, he'd just turned five when Calvin had left. Very few memories remain from that age. Those doubts soon passed as Boyd raced to Calvin and flung his arms around him so tightly James thought he would squeeze the life from him. They stayed like that for some time. Boyd simply wouldn't let go. Calvin enveloped him like a warm blanket, assuring him that he was most definitely home and that they would never be apart again.

The constable suggested a pot of tea all round.

'Good idea,' said James. He turned his attention to the brothers. 'Calvin? Boyd? Why don't you go through to the front room and we'll get some tea sorted.'

Boyd took Calvin's hand and led him to the lounge. James, meanwhile, picked up the telephone receiver and dialled.

'George?'

'James. Something wrong?'

'Just thought you ought to know that Calvin Cameron's put in an appearance.'

'At Cory House?'

'Yes. Can I offer a suggestion?'

George waited.

'Let's go softly softly. Calvin's already said that he's not leaving Boyd, so he's here for a while, suitcase an' all. Your chap is making some tea and I'll have an informal chat with him, see what I can glean and report back. I can then lay the foundations for a formal police visit tomorrow. How does that sound?'

'It sounds like you're sticking your nose in, James. But, to be honest, I think it's a good idea. My constable's still there so he can make sure he doesn't do a runner. But, like you say, I can't imagine he's going far, not as he's just arrived. Find out what you can — particularly when he left India.'

'Right-ho. I say, do you want to join us for dinner at Harrington's tonight? We can go through everything.'

'Yes, that sounds good. Seven o'clock?'

With a time arranged, James booked a table at Harrington's and rang Beth advising her of the arrangements and of the arrival of Calvin Cameron. It took some convincing for her to allow him to chat with Calvin without her.

'Don't you dare hold back on anything when we're at dinner tonight.'

'Darling, I wouldn't dream of it.' He replaced the receiver and joined the Cameron brothers in the front room.

Calvin sat alongside Boyd on the sofa, flicking through the library books that Charlie had just brought in. He high-lighted a number of buildings and statues and clarified what they were, when they were built and what they signified. He caught James' eye; James gestured for him to continue as he sat on an armchair opposite. The police constable brought in a tray, placed it on a side table and prepared a cup and saucer for everyone. Calvin ruffled Boyd's white hair, leant back and spread his arms across the back of the sofa. He closed his eyes and let his head fall back.

James considered him. He was certainly a confident man; perhaps gaining self-reliance from his travels and cutting ties with an overbearing father. Typical of people travelling from sunnier climes, he wore a white linen suit that was severely creased with wear. James cleared his throat and introduced himself formally.

Calvin apologised for not paying him enough attention. 'A shame I had to return in such tragic circumstances.'

'Yes. This is your first trip home since emigrating, is that correct?'

Calvin scanned the room. 'Yes it is and I must admit, I'm surprised to be coming here rather than Yorkshire.' His expression was one of puzzlement. 'What possessed him to move south?'

James apologised for his being forward, but suggested that it might have been to bury old memories. 'I understand that your mother was killed at your previous home. Perhaps that prompted him to want the change.'

The young man gave a wry smile. 'You didn't know my father, Lord Harrington.'

'I confess I didn't, although I did try to welcome him into the village community.'

'And he welcomed you with open arms?'

It was James' turn to smile. Calvin rolled his eyes and reached forward for his tea.

'So much for change.'

'Why do *you* think he moved?'

A perplexed shake of the head provided James with no answers. Calvin reiterated that there had been no love lost between them and, when his mother had been killed, their relationship became more strained.

'What made your father react like that?'

'My father, Lord Harrington, was a ruthless business man. Successful, yes. Rich, undoubtedly. Orderly and efficient, yes. But he was not a man to forge a personal relationship. He met my mother late in life. He loved her, I'm sure, but he was not one to show it. I never saw him provide a tender moment, a loving touch, a word of kindness — nothing. To me and Boyd, she was a vibrant and loving mother. To my father, she was simply his housekeeper and someone to bear children to carry on the family name. Auntie Jeannie probably took over where she left off.'

'But your mother must have known what he was like.'

'I'm sure she did. Perhaps she was trying to escape, too. I don't know. Neither of them spoke of their childhood; father was not someone to confide in anyone. Perhaps mother was providing a love that she never received or was making up for Father's lack of feeling. They muddled along in their own way but things changed once Boyd came along. Father was a religious man, Lord Harrington, but became more so after Mother died. He believed that we are punished by God for any sin. He blamed my mother for how Boyd and I turned out.' He drew Boyd close. 'Boyd's only sin was to be born whiter and purer than snow.' The fondness in his eyes disappeared. 'What sort of man treats an angel like a piece of contaminated dirt?'

Something important streaked through James' mind and disappeared as quickly. He pushed his frustration about it to one side. 'And your wrongdoing?'

Calvin's smile appeared to light up the room. 'Ah, well, that would be telling,

Lord Harrington. I don't know you well enough to divulge.'

James sat back and enjoyed his tea. Here was a man who was exceptionally good-looking, with laughing eyes and a wonderfully caring temperament. He was sure, from speaking with Beth and Kushal, that Calvin had been a womaniser who tested his father's patience and faith with his gallivanting ways.

He decided to change tack. 'I understand you flew back to England?'

Calvin met his gaze. 'Yes, it was certainly much faster than travelling across the ocean. God, that was a monotonous journey all those years ago.'

'Did you fly from Bombay?'

Calvin groaned and described a journey that had taken him all over the place and had begun three days previously; first Delhi, then to Beirut, then to Paris and, finally, to London. He ran his fingers through his thick hair. 'Arrived back today. I have a friend who owns a small plane. He picked me up at Paris and dropped me at Shoreham. Nice little airport, that. It's certainly the way to travel. Have you flown?'

James said he had and that he and Beth often visited France and Italy for their summer break. They chatted about various destinations, their pros and cons and discussed the culture of numerous countries. Boyd snuggled up to Calvin, engrossed in the photographs of beautiful Indian women in silk saris and wise men in turbans. James straightened a seam in his trousers.

'Your wife hasn't travelled with you?'

'No. She never met my family and it's an awful expense to come over for a funeral. The important person in my life is Boyd and she'll meet him soon enough.'

Boyd snuggled in further.

'And you found work in India easy to get?'

'Yes, yes, no problem. My school friend, Josh, had contacts out there, including his cousin, Alastair. So I was fortunate that I found something straight away. And now, of course, Josh and I have our own business.'

'And is business good?'

'India does not stand still. Bombay is a city on the march, Lord Harrington. There's building work going on all the time — it never stops.'

'So, no sudden change of circumstances?'

Calvin's easy-going expression faltered for a split second. In that moment, James detected a hint of melancholy — a sadness that rises up when you least expect it; like a tune that forces you to remember a special time with a special person who is no longer with you. The smile returned as he questioned James' statement. James held his palms up to indicate he meant nothing by it.

'Sometimes businesses hit a peak and then take a downturn,' said James. 'I wondered if you'd been hit with the same? A sudden change that meant you had to rethink things.'

The young man again faltered before he recovered his composure. 'I'm not sure where you're going with these questions, Lord Harrington. But perhaps you could answer a few for me?'

James announced that he'd be glad to.

Calvin slipped his hand inside his jacket pocket and brought out a hip flask.

'First off, do you fancy a whisky? I'm damned sure Father hasn't anything like this here.'

James leapt up and searched the sideboard for two glasses. The bottle of sherry that he'd brought as a welcome gift stood unopened at the back of the cabinet. Calvin tipped out a good measure of whisky for each of them.

'The information I received about these deaths is sketchy,' he said. 'Please, could you fill me in on what's been happening here?'

James hesitated, wondering how much he could divulge. He decided to give him events as any other member of the public would know them. He made a point of quoting what he'd read in the paper and said he assumed the police had things under control.

'The detective on the case, DCI Lane, is a good friend of mine, actually. So he's bound to be knocking on the door tomorrow once he knows you're here.'

Calvin swigged his whisky. 'Not sure

what I can tell him, but I'll certainly do what I can. I didn't get on with Father, or Auntie Jeannie. Neither did a lot of people. But it doesn't mean you want them dead.' He frowned. 'I mean, who would want them dead?'

'You'll have to discuss that with the police. They have questions about that.'

'I haven't seen him for years, but perhaps the cruelty of the man caught up with him. Perhaps he was as cruel to other people as he was to his family. Perhaps he rubbed someone up the wrong way. It makes sense, then, that he would move as far away as possible and carry on as normal.'

'That's a somewhat cynical way of viewing things, Calvin.'

He shrugged. 'You didn't grow up with him as your father. What was your father like?'

James described the quintessential Englishman: upright, fair, supportive and, above all, always there for him and his siblings. Calvin gave a mock bow and stated that he rested his case.

'And Boyd tells me that Father locked

his bedroom door,' continued Calvin. 'What I don't understand is how someone could get in there and kill him.'

Boyd looked up to his brother and whispered that Locksmith Joe was on the run.

James watched Calvin react. His eyes darted here and there as if trying to work something out. His gaze fell on James.

'That man killed my mother.'

James remained silent.

Calvin gave a look of disbelief. 'Well, that's your man,' he said. 'But I don't understand why he'd want to harm Auntie Jeannie. He was off his normal patch. He was robbing our place and got disturbed. It was only Father that saw him. The night that happened, we were upstairs. Is he in this area?'

'So I understand,' said James. 'It's been in the local paper. I believe he may have family nearby.'

Calvin appeared to be processing the information given to him and admitted he was finding it difficult to make sense of it. 'The man must be unhinged. Perhaps he blames us for putting him in jail. If that's the case, the sooner this is cleared up, the better. And the quicker I can take Boyd back to India.'

Boyd's expression was one of pure joy. Calvin ruffled his hair. 'That's right. You and me, Boyd, never to be parted again.'

'Do you think Locksmith Joe somehow got into the house to murder your father?'

'I can't imagine they call him Locksmith Joe for nothing,' said Calvin. 'If he can get into a locked room, he can get out and lock it again, don't you think?'

'But the key was still in the lock,' said James. 'Your aunt had to ask the postman to break the door down.'

Calvin glanced at him. 'Well perhaps he had an ingenious way of replacing the key.'

'Unless there's a secret passage,' James said with a wry smile.

The young man started. 'I think you're leaping into the imagination of a Hollywood producer.'

James had a flashback to the smuggling tunnels he'd found during the summer. 'Would you mind if I indulged in those imaginings?'

He felt Calvin scrutinise his motives and then the warm smile returned. 'Why not? Let's both go up and see what we can find. Lead the way.'

Cory House was gradually being refreshed. Christie Cameron had ordered work that would be ongoing for several months. Nothing too decorative but it was surprising what a coat of paint did for the place. But his own room had yet to be touched. In short, Christie Cameron's room was spartan. One wardrobe, one chest of drawers, a wooden chair, a sink, a single bed and a wooden cross. A rug covered part of the floorboards and a faded nativity scene hung on the wall. Calvin suggested James take one side and he take the other.

'Not much to show for a life, is it?'

James had to agree there was little there. They scanned the room and knocked on walls. Some sounded muffled, some hollow, but there was nothing to suggest any secret passageways: no built-in shelves with a trigger book title, no hidden switches or levers and nothing suspicious behind the wardrobe.

'Disappointed, Lord Harrington?'

James afforded him a bashful smile. 'It would have been nice, though, wouldn't it?'

They made their way back to the living room. The front door opened and a voice rang out.

'Hello.'

A moment later, Suzie peered round the edge of the living room door. She spotted Calvin and, at first looked blank. Slowly, her mouth dropped open and her eyes widened in shock. 'Calvin?'

The young man smiled at Suzie who then screamed his name and dashed across to hug him. James took this as his cue to leave and let the family reacquaint themselves with one another. He bade them goodbye and promised to drop in another time. In the hallway, Lucy was struggling with two bags of shopping. James dashed forward to help her carry them into the kitchen. She swept a stray hair from her face.

'What's all the noise about?'

'Calvin's back.'

He received an incredulous stare. Then she gazed down the hall.

'Oh, but . . . ' She checked her watch. 'Goodness.'

She smoothed her skirt, teased her hair and skipped down the hall and into the front room. James shrugged his jacket on and opened the front door. Boyd slipped alongside him and tugged his sleeve.

'What is it, Boyd?'

'Did you get my letters?'

'I did. Was it you who left them?'

He shook his head.

'Do you know who did?'

He remained silent.

'Do you want them back?'

Another shake of the head.

'Do you want me to read them?'

Boyd's pink eyes glistened. There was vulnerability there; as if he had the worries of the world bearing down on his young frame. He raced back to Calvin.

James closed the door behind him and stood on the top step, deep in thought. What on earth was that about? Something was disturbing Boyd — something to do with the letters. What could that be? Perhaps talking this through with Beth and George would clarify things a little better.

18

The floral display in reception received a good many compliments from the guests at Harrington's. It was 7 p.m., the gong had sounded for dinner and well-to-do couples and families made their way through to the dining area.

James, sporting a pristine black suit and light-blue striped tie, stood back to allow their guests through to the dining room. Beth, in black swing-trousers and a rust-brown twinset, linked arms with him. They followed the guests through and took their table by one of the windows with views toward the South Downs. Adam, their head waiter, noted their drinks order and announced he'd return for their meal selection once Mr Lane had arrived. Five minutes later, George strode into the room, his trilby in one hand and a buff-coloured folder in the other. He dragged a chair out.

'Sorry I'm late. Lost track of time.'

'We've ordered a beer for you, is that all right?' said James.

George's grateful smile answered his question. His friend sat down and picked up the menu. 'Steak and kidney pudding? Well, I think that's got my name written on it.'

Beth said that it was Grandma Harrington's special recipe. 'They'll have been steaming the ingredients all afternoon.'

'She's not wrong, George,' said James. 'I remember my grandmother preparing this in the kitchen. Chopped everything up, sprinkled it with flour and gravy powder and let it steam in its own juices. Absolutely glorious. I think I'm going to join you on that one. How about you, Beth?'

'To be honest, I can't argue with your choice.'

Adam delivered two beers and a glass of Babycham and then took their order. They chinked their glasses and chorused 'Cheers'.

George shrugged his jacket off and straightened his tie. 'Well, this beats a ham sandwich at the station.'

'Shame you couldn't join us yesterday,' said James. 'Our friend, Patel, talked Beth through preparing a rather lovely chicken curry. He brought the spices down with him. I must say, I was rather taken with it.'

'Sounds exotic,' replied George. 'He's an insightful chap, isn't he? I got to know him quite well over the last couple of days and he certainly knows how to speak to people, no matter where they're from or what they do.'

James sipped the froth off the top of his bitter and agreed, commenting on what an asset he must have been during the war. He placed his glass on the table.

'So, how is the finest of the force this evening?'

George struggled to retrieve the contents of his inside jacket pocket. They waited patiently until he finally brought out an envelope.

'Hah, here we are. A few people took some photographs at the festival and we had all the films developed.' He slid them across the table. 'Do either of you see anything untoward or someone you don't recognise?'

James shared the prints with Beth and discussed the images. Most were taken along the route as the scarecrows were making their way toward the village green. They shared a laugh at the costumes and the expressions of the residents. Beth picked out one photograph.

'Oh, this is a lovely one of Charlie's children. Are these his photographs?'

'His and Graham Porter's. We had others, but they were just family photos — no crowd scenes.'

'Ah ha,' said James. 'This, I believe, is young Boyd.'

The black and white photographs showed the majority of scarecrow entrants dancing behind the band. At the side, a number of spectators were viewing the parade; including Boyd who had dressed in a moth-eaten jacket and a floppy hat and sported a lopsided moustache and sideburns.

Beth narrowed her eyes. 'How can you tell that's him?'

'His shoes. He was wearing them up at Cory House. I think they must be a favourite pair or something. He'd drawn pictures on the toes — you can just make them out.'

Beth and George examined the photo

as James continued leafing through the rest. 'A-ha!' He pulled out another print. 'Here's Jeannie Cameron. See her expression.'

Beth peered in. 'Goodness, she looks furtive.'

'And this is before she reached the marquee. This is still in the high street.' James flicked through some more images and snatched one out. 'Here. This is the man I saw. Jeannie gaped at him as if she'd seen a ghost.'

'Sweetie, she must have arranged to meet him. Why else would she be there?'

George took the image from him and squinted. 'Not very clear, is it?'

'No, it's not and it's not face on, either. But you can see a bushy beard and he's pretty bulky. Do you think he's Locksmith Joe?'

His friend shrugged. 'Got the right build.'

James tidied the photos together and handed them back. 'Not a great deal of help then. Sorry, old chap. You were rather pinning your hopes on those.'

'George,' said Beth, 'have you spoken to the local paper? They took some photographs.'

George tapped his nose with his index finger, opened the folder and brought out several wide-angled shots of the festival parade as it arrived on the green. James took them and he and Beth examined the prints. One, in particular, caught his eye.

'Here he is again, I think. He's coming in from the opposite end to the parade. It's not terribly clear.'

'The road leading past this place,' observed George. 'You haven't got him stashed away here, have you?' he said with a glint in his eye.

James grinned and continued checking the photograph. He couldn't help but feel frustrated. 'He's certainly camera shy. If he approached the village from this direction, he's either holed up near Charnley or camping in our woods.'

George took the prints from him and replaced them in the folder. 'D'you mind if I send a few officers over tomorrow? Just to check? We'll dress 'em up so they don't look like coppers.'

James spread his hands to indicate his permission.

'You said that this Locksmith Joe chap

killed Gwen Cameron in a robbery gone wrong. Why on earth would he want the rest of the Camerons killed?'

'Yes, I'm struggling with that one. Perhaps this is some sort of revenge thing. I had a chat with one of the prison officers today who said Joe always claimed it wasn't him; that he was serving time for something he didn't do. And he was a model prisoner, never any trouble.'

'But surely,' Beth put in, 'he'd be best putting his efforts toward clearing his name?'

'You'd think so, wouldn't you? I've spoken to the prison officials and there doesn't seem to be anything deranged about the man. But, you never know what people are thinking. Until we find him, we're keeping a police presence at Cory House.' He inclined his head. 'Which brings us nicely to your visit there today.'

Adam arrived with three plates of steak and kidney pudding, mashed potatoes with a medley of wild mushrooms and runner beans from the Harrington estate. The enticing smell of beef juices and gravy prompted them to delay their discussion.

James' fork halved the feather-light suet and the kidneys were as soft as sponge. The steak fell apart and the gravy, mixed with onions, was thick and beefy.

In the corner of the room, the pianist played a soothing nocturne by Chopin.

Near the end of his meal, James put his cutlery down and dabbed the corners of his mouth with a napkin. He picked up his beer and took a short sip to clear the palate.

'Calvin Cameron is an extremely likeable young man. Not knowing him before puts me at a disadvantage, of course. Although he didn't elaborate, he hinted at having been a rebellious child; certainly a rebellious teenager.'

Beth asked, 'Do you think his behaviour involved girls?'

'I'm almost certain of it, yes. But how to find out if anything untoward happened? I wouldn't know where to start.'

'Untoward, for Christie Cameron, could mean seeing Calvin simply looking at a girl.'

George marshalled suet and kidney onto his fork. 'I'll see what I can dig up. If he got a girl in the family way, there must be a record of it somewhere.'

'Not necessarily, old chap. If the respective families wanted to cover the whole thing up, I'm sure they could. If there was a child, he or she could be living abroad.'

His friend grunted. He swallowed the last of his dinner and pushed his plate back a couple of inches. 'Right, James, let's take it from the beginning.' He picked up the pepper pot. 'Christie Cameron, cantankerous and overbearing, moves from Otley to Cavendish, where he knows no one. Why?'

'Calvin suggested that he might have upset someone in Yorkshire.'

'Enough to move so far south?'

Beth slid her own plate away. 'A coward's way out?'

George placed the pepper pot down. 'Did Calvin have any other thoughts?'

'Not really. He seemed pretty stumped about the whole thing himself.' James felt for his cigarettes. 'Have you found out much about Christie your end?'

George let them know that Christie

Cameron didn't have a criminal record of any kind. The only information the police had, emerged at the time of the murder of his wife: he had come across as being moody and stubborn, as well as somewhat derogatory about his wife.

Beth tut-tutted. 'That's dreadful. The man didn't seem to have a caring bone in his body. It makes you wonder how he managed to have children.'

James turned, surprised at her forthright observation, but highlighted something that Calvin had said. 'An off-the-cuff remark really, but suggesting that Christie married to ensure he had an heir.' He turned to George. 'Sounds rather harsh, doesn't it?'

'Especially as he turned against those heirs. Did Calvin go into much there?'

Adam approached and asked permission to clear the table. When he had done so, he left the dessert menus with Beth. James picked up the salt pot.

'Christie blamed Mrs Cameron for bringing a child into the world that was not perfect.' He heard Beth catch her breath. 'And Calvin appears to have gone off the rails. If this isn't Locksmith Joe and you're considering the family as suspects, anger could be a motive. Calvin was angry at his father for the way he treated them. Lucy and Suzie are both angry over the treatment of Boyd.'

'You think they're all in it together?'

James shrugged. 'But who had access to Christie's room? Jeannie Cameron, certainly. I'm not sure that Boyd had. Christie didn't seem to want the boy near him. I even resorted to hunting for a secret passage today.'

George and Beth stared. He shrugged. 'I found nothing. Calvin came up with me. We knocked on walls, tried to turn taps and doorknobs to find secret handles, but all to no avail.'

Beth sat forward and linked her fingers together. 'Jeannie blamed Boyd for killing Christie, but do you think she meant as a process over the years? It seems that, after Gwen Cameron died, Christie became bitter, stricter in his beliefs. Without Gwen, who Suzie suggested was a loving mother, something ate into Christie.'

George nodded slowly. 'That's a good point.'

'Jeannie Cameron,' said James, 'appeared to be more of a housekeeper than a sister. Do you think there was some resentment there? Could they have moved to Cavendish and she was thinking it was a new start? Yet there she was, back to being his skivvy. Perhaps that took her over the edge and she drugged and smothered him.' He picked up the dessert menu. 'After all, she did seem a little potty herself.'

Beth peeked over his shoulder at the menu. 'But then, who killed her?'

'The pair of you are forgetting something,' said George. 'Locksmith Joe. He picks locks. He's connected to that family.'

James groaned. 'But why kill Jeannie Cameron? I mean, was she definitely in the house when Gwen Cameron was killed?'

George gave a despondent shrug. 'Yes, she was, but she didn't see anything. It makes no sense. I want to believe this convict is guilty. I don't like the coincidence that he escapes just as the Camerons move down here. That's too convenient. And, like you say, Beth, if he wants to clear his name, what's he doing going around killing people?'

Adam approached and took their dessert order: three pear tarts with chocolate sauce. James leant back.

'Then, of course, we have the inheritance. Both Calvin and Boyd — and the two cousins — come off rather nicely from these deaths.' He sat up. 'I say, you don't think they know Locksmith Joe, do you?'

George looked quizzical. James held his hands up in surrender. 'Yes, perhaps that's a little farfetched.'

'I'm sure Locksmith Joe's still in the area,' said George. 'We had a few sightings a couple of days ago, but he's doing a good job of hiding.'

James reached across and nudged Beth, bringing her out of her daydream. 'What are you thinking, darling?'

'Just trying to make sense of it all.'

George stretched back. 'It's difficult, isn't it? If Christie Cameron was so against his wife and seemingly abhorred his children, why did he leave them such a huge inheritance?' He massaged the back of his neck. 'Something must have happened, because the will was changed earlier in the year. Before, he'd not included Calvin in the will and had set Boyd up to go into an institution. It was changed so that every-thing went to the boys and the nieces.'

James reminded them that, going by his letters, Calvin's marriage would have built bridges with his father. 'It sounds as if this coincided with Calvin's wedding.'

George dragged his chair closer with an expression of exasperation. 'What letters?'

James groaned. He'd forgotten that George didn't know. He hesitatingly described the package that had arrived and the letters contained therein.

George gritted his teeth. 'And when did you intend to tell me about these?'

The relationship between them was a good one but, every now and again, James felt like the pupil to George's headmaster. This was one of those occasions.

'Someone sent them to me and asked me to keep them safe. We've read them through, only briefly, haven't we, darling?' Beth agreed. 'They appear to be updates from one brother to another, that's all.'

'Could I possibly be the judge of that?' said George. 'That could be vital evidence.'

Adam delivered the tarts and Beth

scooped up her spoon and fork. 'Oh George, stop being a fuddy-duddy. Don't you think we would have shown you if there was something incriminating?'

'It's evidence,' insisted George. 'And who are you two to decide what's relevant and what isn't?'

'He's got a point, darling,' said James. 'George, why don't I pack them all up tomorrow and bring them over?'

'Why were they sent to you in the first place?'

James rotated his plate. 'I've no idea. I'm not even sure that I was supposed to read them, but my sleuthing head got the better of me. I skimmed through most of them because they seemed to be just news from India.' He scooped a small piece of tart and chocolate cream onto his spoon. 'There were a couple of things that struck me as odd this afternoon.'

He was aware that all eyes were upon him as he brought his spoon up.

'Boyd appeared vulnerable,' he continued. 'It's as if he felt there was something odd going on. I mean, he's a timid boy at the best of times, but I sensed an underlying fear or anxiety of some sort.'

George grimaced. 'Christ, James, you'll cost me my job. I'll let you have those letters for one more day. See what you can glean from them. Then you hand them over.'

James made a mental note of the days. 'That takes us to Sunday. It's Harvest Festival — are you attending Stephen's service? I believe he's also conducting a small remembrance for the Camerons, so it may be worth your while.'

'Yeah, he told me. I'll pop in and see if I can observe anything suspicious. Not that I've ever seen anyone suspicious at funerals and services. I think that just happens in the films.'

In ten minutes, they'd polished off the pear tarts and had moved on to a small glass of port each to complete the meal. George prepared his pipe.

'You said there were a couple of things that struck you as odd this afternoon. You only gave me one.'

James waved his cigarette smoke away from the table. 'Yes, the other thing was when Lucy arrived. I told her that Calvin was here and she had a certain demeanour about her.'

'What d'you mean?' asked Beth.

'Something in her behaviour. It was as if she wasn't expecting him just yet. She seemed a little flustered and started teasing her hair as if she were . . . '

Beth's eyes gleamed. 'As if she were preparing to flirt with him.'

He snapped his fingers. 'Yes, that's exactly what it was like.'

'Goodness, do you think she has designs on him?'

'Well, if she has, she needs to remind herself that he's married. I say, do you have anything on the girls, George?'

His friend made a face to indicate he had nothing. 'Seem pretty normal. We made a few enquiries at their workplaces and they knuckle down, work hard, don't have any troubles. The girls said they struggled with rent and bills and they pay them at the last minute. Not frivolous with money. No criminal records. Lived in Shoreham until their parents died and now live in a flat in Hove. Pokey accommodation, but it's all they can afford.'

James suggested that a windfall wouldn't go amiss where the girls were concerned. Adam approached and presented the bill on a silver salver. James pulled out his wallet and paid, asking for compliments to go to Didier. He was aware of George's bemused expression. His friend had commented after a previous engagement that he couldn't believe James was paying for a meal in his own hotel. But he'd made a point of doing that since Harrington's opened. Taking free meals and drinks simply went against the grain.

Ten minutes later, they said goodbye to George and watched his car disappear down the drive. James opened the passenger door of the Austin Healey for Beth. A movement in the shadows caught his eye. He stopped and stared at a clump of trees across the grass. Someone was beckoning him over. He frowned. Beth wound the window down.

'What's up, sweetie?'

'Stay here. I'll be two minutes.'

It was a clear night and the chill of autumn struck him as he approached the trees. He wrapped his suit jacket around him. He hadn't anticipated walking across a field and wished he'd put an overcoat on. He scanned the area.

'Psst.'

James turned and closed his eyes in relief.

'Bert, what the hell are you doing here?'

Bert crept out from the darkness and sheepishly slid his cap off. He screwed it up in his hands.

James clapped his hands together. 'Right, what's all the cloak and dagger stuff about?'

His friend fidgeted and struggled to keep eye contact.

'I say, Bert, whatever is it? You know you can tell me.'

Bert shifted his attention skyward, then met James' gaze and blurted out. 'I'm looking after Locksmith Joe. He's in the woods on your estate.'

'What?' James didn't know whether to punch him or lecture him. 'Why here? Why on the estate? Good heavens, Bert, you're harbouring a criminal.'

'Hear me out. If you walk away once

you've heard what I've gotta say, so be it. But, hear me out.'

James let out a frustrated sigh. He and Bert had a long-standing friendship but the man infuriated him at times.

'I never 'elped him escape,' Bert said. 'But I knew he was being sprung. His mum's elderly, she lives the other side of Lewes. His family's in Bognor. I'm the only bloke he knows around here, so I offered to shelter 'im.'

'All this so he can see his mother?'

'No, mate. Nothing to do with her, she just told me he was being sprung. He's not a killer, Jimmy boy. He wouldn't hurt a fly. Joe's one of the nicest blokes you'll ever meet. He'd rob you blind, yes, but he'd never hurt you.'

'Bert, everyone is capable of killing. When Beth was taken last year, I would have killed to protect her.'

A branch snapped.

They turned.

Out of the gloom came a large, bulky man with a bushy beard and a floppy hat. James raised his eyes heavenward.

'Locksmith Joe, I believe.'

James allowed himself a wry smile as the man bowed.

'Guv'nor.' He spoke in a similar Cockney accent to Bert but a little more deeply. 'I'm sorry I've caused problems. I'll move on tomorrow if you want me to. I followed Bert. I wanted to hear what you had to say.'

'What I have to say, Joe, is that you should turn yourself in. You're not doing yourself any favours.'

'That ain't gonna 'appen,' said Bert. 'Not until he's done what 'e has to do.'

'And what is that, Bert? What can he possibly do that will make this remotely easier for him?' James moved forward to join his friend. 'Do you have any idea of the position you're putting me in?'

'Hear us out, that's all I'm asking.'

Locksmith Joe came closer. 'I wanna clear my name, Lord Harrington.'

'But you were seen killing Mrs Cam — '

'No.' Joe grabbed his arm. James flinched. The old boy backed off slightly. 'I didn't kill that Mrs Cameron, Lord Harrington. Christie Cameron killed his wife. I saw 'im do it. I was set up.'

James stared into the man's pleading eyes. He didn't know what to think; having an escaped prisoner suddenly turn up out of the blue had thrown him off track.

He turned in frustration to Bert. 'I can't do this now, Bert. Beth's in the car, it's late. I'll borrow my gardener's Land Rover and come to you tomorrow. Where's he hiding out?'

'Two fields back. In the clearing of the woods back there, about 'undred yards in.'

'I'll be there at ten o'clock tomorrow morning.'

He watched as the pair of them disappeared into the trees and realised his heart was thumping nineteen to the dozen. He didn't know whether to be livid with Bert or commend him for standing by a friend. He marched across the lawn toward his car. There was only one thing he was sure of. The mystery surrounding Christie and Jeannie Cameron had taken an unexpected turn and thrown up all sorts of new questions.

19

The Land Rover bumped and swerved as James drove across the fields behind Harrington's. It was not unusual for him to borrow the vehicle to make an inspection of the land and surrounding fences, so no one was surprised to see him take off in his tweed jacket and traditional flat cap. Beth had hugged him goodbye, promising to stay quiet until his return. Later that day, they would return Kushal to Richmond but, for this morning, the Indian was spending time with GJ to impart as much information as possible to the young man about the mother he never knew.

The gold and red leaves of autumn blended with the pale blue cloudless sky. Rabbits scurried across the field to the side of him. Ahead was a small wood where, decades ago, the foresters lit their charcoal burners. He manoeuvred the Land Rover through the trees and parked as far into the wood as he could. He pulled a small rucksack from the passenger seat and checked his watch. It was ten o'clock precisely. He swung the rucksack over his shoulder and strode deeper into the forest toward the clearing. Two minutes later, he saw Bert waving. He acknowledged the wave and threaded his way through the undergrowth.

Joe had set up a small tent with a piece of green tarpaulin. James guessed the man had regular army training as it appeared well constructed and professionally camouflaged. It inclined slightly to allow for rainfall. The old man poured tea from a Thermos flask that James presumed Bert had supplied. His friend pointed to a tree stump where James sat down and tossed the rucksack to Joe. He opened it gingerly, then delved inside and brought out a tin-opener, a tiny calor gas stove, a small frying pan, some bacon and a tin of baked beans. A grateful smile spread across his face.

'Blimey. Thanks, guv'nor.'

Bert's astonishment was not lost on James. He shrugged. 'He's here now, so the least I can do is make sure he doesn't starve to death.' He accepted a bottle of lemonade from Bert and took a swig. 'I hope what you're going to tell me is good, otherwise I shan't have any choice but to call George in.'

Joe's ears pricked. 'George? Who's he?'

'DCI Lane. His officers have been searching for you.'

Bert sat on the ground and leant back against a tree. 'He's an old friend, Joe. He won't have any choice.'

Joe screwed the top back onto the flask. 'Right, I'd best make a start then.' He faced James. 'I was in Yorkshire with two mates. First time I'd ever been there. They 'ad a job on, a bank job. They 'ad two drivers. One as a lookout, one as a getaway. One of the drivers had let 'em down, so they asked me to keep watch. That's all I did. Parked up by the bank and kept a lookout. If I saw anything dodgy, I was to toot the horn three times and drive away. Anyways, they did the job, no problem.

'I met up with 'em that night and there were some other people there. They starts talking about robberies they'd done and some of the big 'ouses in the area. Then they starts talking about that Cameron bloke. That he's rolling in it.' He took a slurp of tea. 'So I finds out where this bloke lives. I figured that, if he's rolling in it, I'd nick a couple o' nice pieces that he wouldn't miss.'

He sat upright.

'I weren't gonna pinch lots. Just a few things.'

James' lips tightened. 'If you're trying to justify your living, you're failing miserably.'

Joe shrugged. 'One of the geezers involved in the bank robbery gave me a camera by way of a payment. He knew the way I operated for people, taking pictures and all. An Exakta it was, right good little camera. Told me to get in there and take some pictures of any antiques on show. If there were, they said they might get over there and do the place over 'emselves.'

'You really have no qualms about any of this, do you?'

'That night,' continued Joe unabashed,

'I got a bus to where he lived. Outside of Bradford it was, place called Otley — easy to find. I had a torch with me and I waited until it was proper dark before I did anything. They had two young lads there; one was more a toddler and they were put to bed. I saw the lights go out in their rooms. I got in a bit closer and could see through the kitchen window. I 'ad the camera ready, but I had to wait for them to go upstairs before I could get in. The flash would 'ave given me away.'

He slurped more tea.

'Well, I sat on the grass for ages and they starts 'aving an argument.'

'The Camerons?'

'Yeah. They were going at it like hammer and tongs. Right argy-bargy there was.'

'Do you know what about?'

'Not really. Got little snippets 'ere and there, but I couldn't make no sense of it. Anyway, I got up and peered through the window. That Cameron bloke was pretty sturdy, quite muscular, but she was having none of his lip and slapped 'im round the face.'

He let out a silent phew.

'When she did that, Cameron got up — stood tall over her, and put his 'ands around her throat. I couldn't believe it. She started choking, spluttering, trying to claw him off, but he kept squeezing. Her eyes were bulging and she went red in the face. I don't know what made me do it, but I got the camera and snapped a picture and then all 'ell broke loose.'

James sat forward.

'He let 'er fall to the ground cos, by then, I'd busted through the door. I pushed Cameron to one side and went to pick 'is wife up. Take her away.'

'She was still alive?' asked James.

'Oh yes,' said Joe, a hint of anger behind the statement. 'She was struggling to breathe but, yeah, she was alive.'

'Then what?'

'Then I got knocked out. Out cold I was. When I came to, I 'ad handcuffs on and 'is wife was dead. The police 'ad come out. Cameron said I'd broken in and demanded money and threatened to kill 'em.' His voice was shaky. 'I wouldn't 'ave done that. Cameron said he went to get money and, when he got back, he found his wife dead and that I then attacked him. He said he hit me with a saucepan in self-defence.' A tear fell down his cheek. 'I didn't touch 'em, guv'nor. I did nothing wrong. I didn't even nick anything.'

The silence that followed was a welcome one. Bert moved across to Joe and put an arm around him. Joe brushed away tears that kept falling.

James watched him. He hated to admit it, but his instinct was telling him to believe this man. Instinct invariably was correct. How many times had he gone to do one thing and allowed logic to take over, only to discover that his initial decision had been correct? He gazed at the canopy of autumn leaves above him and then at Joe.

'I take it this camera never materialised?'

A shake of the head supported his statement. Joe sniffed and wiped the last of his tears away. 'I've no chance now, have I? Now he's dead.'

'Did you see his sister, Jeannie

Cameron, in the house?'

'I didn't see anyone else except the boys going to their room. If she was there, I never saw her.'

'So this was your word against Christie Cameron?'

'I didn't stand a chance.'

James pondered the scenario. The word of a wealthy businessman against a known robber; it was clear why the verdict went as it did.

'Was there any evidence against you?'

'My pockets were stuffed with some notes. I didn't put 'em there, though.'

Bert slapped Joe on the back and wandered across to James. 'What d'you think?'

James stood up and brushed himself down. 'His innocence depends on whether Christie kept that camera.'

'That's not likely, is it?'

'I'm not so sure. There are killers who like the idea of a memento or a punishment.'

'Punishment?'

'Christie Cameron was a God-fearing man. The act of killing someone would have gone against everything he stood for. Placing blame on an innocent man, again, contradicts the essence of who he was. He may well have kept the camera to punish himself, torment himself about the ultimate sin. His own son commented on how strictly he followed his faith after his wife died.'

Bert took it all in slowly. 'Sounds a bit like that farmer whose death you investigated last year.' He pushed his cap back. 'So, what now? He can't give 'imself up. They'll cart 'im back to Wandsworth and throw away the key.'

'He'll need to move from here. George is sending some officers to scour the woods later today. I don't want to know where you take him. The less I know the better. But please, not on my land.'

His friend's face lit up. 'I knew you'd hear me out.'

'We have to trust that he kept that camera,' continued James. 'Cory House is devoid of ornaments and nick-nacks. If he had it, it would be easy to find. My fear is that he discarded it when he left Yorkshire. A new start, so to speak.'

'You'll look, though.'

James said that, yes, he would. He poked Bert in the chest. 'You, meanwhile, have been conspicuous by your absence. Even George was wondering where you were. I know you're concerned about Joe, but you must act normally. Are you coming to the Harvest Festival tomorrow?'

'I weren't,' replied Bert. 'But, now you've said all that, I s'pose I'd better.'

'Good chap.' James checked his watch and wandered over to Joe. 'Bert is shifting you somewhere else, Joe. I'll be in touch via him.'

Joe offered him his hand. 'Thanks, guv'nor.'

James went to go, but turned. 'I say, were you at the scarecrow festival in the village?'

'Yeah, I was. I remember bringing my nippers to see it years ago. I wanted to see it for old times' sake. I watched the parade go by and came back 'ere. I didn't go near the tent, though.'

'You didn't see anyone else dressed similarly to you?'

The convict's quizzical stare answered his question.

Ten minutes later, James' Land Rover emerged from the woods. Goodness, what on earth would George say if he knew? And where did this leave the investigation? He sent up a silent prayer as he pulled out onto the main road.

'Please Lord, don't let George find out that Bert's shielding Locksmith Joe.'

★   ★   ★

On arriving home, he learnt that Kushal had already taken his leave. He watched Beth as she prepared tea.

'He and GJ hit it off magnificently and the pair of them returned to Richmond. I think Kushal has some old photographs of Delphine Brooks-Hunter, so GJ offered to take him home. He also went to sit with Boyd and assure him that he can always contact him. They've established quite a bond. It's a shame, you've just missed him.'

'Yes, I'll telephone him later to thank him for coming down. I'm pleased that he's seeing Boyd again — the lad will get a lot of confidence from that.'

She poured boiling water into the teapot. 'How was your inspection?'

'The less you know, the better.'

'I guess from that comment you are not reporting this to George.'

James put his arms around her waist. 'Not yet. That probably doesn't sit comfortably with you.'

'Not really. Is he still on our land?'

'Bert's moving him on.'

She swivelled round to face him and poked him gently on the chest. 'I'll not mention it again unless you want to discuss it, but be careful. That man is a criminal, a killer.'

'I'm not so sure he is, darling.' He fondled her fingers. 'Let me think on this for a while. I'll go through it with you later.'

'I'll look forward to it. In the meantime, Stephen and Anne are on their way. Anne for a chat, but Stephen wants to discuss the Camerons' remembrance service. I think he wants a bit of reassurance.'

James chuckled. 'I would have agreed if he had to deliver it to Christie and Jeannie. I can't imagine Boyd and Calvin getting upset about the content of his speech.'

The doorbell rang. Beth untied her apron and hung it on the back of the kitchen door. 'That'll be them. Would you mind taking that teapot through? Everything else is in the lounge.'

James gave her a mock salute and took the said teapot through, while Beth ushered Stephen and Anne in.

'Ah, hello,' said James in welcome. 'I don't seem to have seen you for a while. Did Luke and Mark enjoy the scarecrow festival?'

Anne described two very excited children who were so looking forward to it that they hadn't been able to sleep. 'And now we have the Harvest Festival, which I've been counting the days to. It's such an uplifting celebration.'

They took their seats and Beth played mother while Anne distributed a selection of butterfly cakes.

'M-Mr Patel gone?' asked Stephen.

Beth repeated her explanation to the Merryweathers. Anne perched on the edge of the sofa.

'And how's the investigation going?'

'Stuttering, I think is the word I would use,' replied James. 'Even George is having problems. But, that aside, I believe your reason for visiting is to run the remembrance ideas past me. Let's resolve that before we move on to any other business.'

Anne sighed. 'I've heard this too many times, Stephen. I don't know why you're worrying about it.'

Beth suggested that she and Anne go into the study. 'Catherine dropped the patterns by for the bridesmaid dresses.'

'Oh, that sounds much more enjoyable.'

They took a selection of cakes and grabbed their cups and saucers and, within a minute, were ensconced next door.

Stephen fidgeted and couldn't seem to settle.

'Stephen, I'm sure that whatever you're going to say will be fine,' said James. 'Let's put things into perspective. You're not doing the funeral. Boyd and Calvin are not Christie Cameron. I'm not entirely sure they're terribly religious. Suzie and Lucy don't strike me as the sort of people to take offence. It's not as if either Christie or his sister was well-liked. And no one knew them in Cavendish. What exactly is it that frets you?'

'I-I think it's that I know what h-he was like. I feel that he'll be listening to everything I s-say tomorrow.'

James laughed. 'And strike you down if he disapproves? Really Stephen, I think you're getting worked up over nothing. You've only to say a couple of lines. No one is expecting anything more. It's Harvest Festival. That's your main focus for tomorrow.'

Stephen brightened and placed his hands on his knees. 'Y-you're right. I-I had composed a long, drawn-out speech about the Camerons, but it would be inappropriate. A few lines. Yes. That's all I n-need.'

James reached across to the shoebox of letters. 'I say, you don't fancy having a rummage through some of these, do you?'

He confided in Stephen that he'd been sent the letters and wondered if the reverend would see anything that he and Beth hadn't.

'W-why not? It'll pass an hour while the wives are c-conspiring.'

James leafed through the envelopes. 'I thought I'd concentrate on the last year to eighteen months. I feel sure something happened. Kushal suggested it when we read through them a couple of days ago. Everything was going well until Calvin appeared and he seems keen that Boyd join him in India straight away.'

'And has Calvin i-indicated any urgency?'

James said he hadn't and joined Stephen on the sofa. They read through several letters that simply offered snippets of information on Bombay, Calvin's accommodation, the sights, the sounds and smells, the bars he frequented and the people he'd met. A number had photographs enclosed of elephants and exotic birds.

The letters went from handwritten to typewritten and expressed much the same message. Stephen went to hand the second typewritten letter back, but reread it. James waited patiently as his friend dragged a finger across the paper.

'I-I think this is a telling phrase.'

'What's that?'

' 'I cannot live a lie. It's s-surprising how powerful love is.' '

James took the letter from him. For the most part, it was the same as the other letters, with updates and experiences. However, he thought that he may as well read the one part that had caught Stephen's eye.

' 'Boyd, I am not being true to myself. Perhaps the Camerons are cursed. It certainly seems that way. I cannot live a lie, though. It's surprising how powerful love is.' '

He folded the letter and replaced it in the box. 'You think this is to do with love?'

'L-love, acceptance, support, th-the respect of your e-elders,' replied Stephen. 'Perhaps an inappropriate affair? He's married a respectable girl. I-I can't imagine his father disapproving of that. But has he married that girl for his f-father? Was he in love with someone else?'

'Actually, I believe he may have been. Beth seems to think Lucy was in love with him. So you think Calvin married for convenience to gain the love of his father?'

'D-don't you? It w-wouldn't be the first time such a thing has happened.'

James flicked through the envelopes and retrieved those with photographs in. 'You know, he sent over snapshots of his wife, but none of them together.' He turned to Stephen. 'I wonder if he ever did marry?'

'O-only one way to find out.'

James agreed, but suggested it would be a difficult conversation and that he was far too distant from the family to ask it. 'Calvin seems an easygoing chap, but I think even he would draw the line at me questioning his marriage.'

A light-bulb moment appeared to give Stephen a lift. 'W-what about your friend at Somerset House? Will he have contacts in India who can find out for you? Y-you have approximate dates and a city. Th-there can't be th-that many Calvin Camerons getting married in Bombay.'

'You're certainly on the ball, Merry-weather.' James leapt up and opened the bureau in the corner of the room to retrieve his address book. 'Ah yes, here we are. Gerald Crabtree.'

Gerald Crabtree had access to records of births, marriages and deaths at Somerset House. He'd helped James in the past when trying to sort out GJ's little mystery. James dashed out to the telephone in the hall and, five minutes later, returned with a smile on his face.

'Merryweather, you are a genius. He *does* have contacts in Bombay. He's going to see what he can rustle up.'

Beth and Anne joined them and James updated the pair on their interpretation of the letters and the phone call to London. Beth clasped her hands together. 'How exciting.'

'And intriguing,' said Anne.

James shut the lid on the shoebox and offered to refill the teapot. In the kitchen, a doubt crossed his mind. Even if Calvin was living a lie, how would this have affected the events here in Cavendish? Had Christie and Jeannie discovered

Calvin's secret? He agitated the tea leaves in the pot.

That would certainly create a motive for murder, he thought to himself. That, and the fact that Calvin would inherit a considerable sum of money.

20

The sun cast a pale light across Cavendish as villagers made their way toward St Nicholas' church. It was a still day and the autumnal chill was a refreshing one.

James pulled up a short distance from the village green and leapt out to open the car door for Beth. He wore a grey suit, a Crombie coat and a trilby. Beth had opted for a gold tweed skirt with a matching jacket. She'd chosen a petite feather and lace hat and court shoes. He opened the boot and brought out a wooden box full of parsnips, onions, potatoes and flowers. They made their way across the village green and toward the church. The bells pealed a welcome to all.

Stephen, in his Sunday robes, greeted his congregation like long-lost friends as they filed past to take their place in the pews, each adult and child laden with harvest gifts. Flowers, vegetables and fruit were predominantly held by the adults, while tins of soup and packets of flour and cereal were carried in by the children.

James and Beth exchanged greetings with Stephen before making their way inside. At the front, Anne guided each individual to a particular area to lay their offering down.

'Oh, goodness, everyone has been so generous,' she said as she manoeuvred them toward a side wall. 'I think we'll put your things there.'

They took a second to admire the church. The harvest gifts themselves were placed with care to ensure they could all be seen. Seasonal sprays were carefully interspersed with root vegetables and larder foods. The display appeared busy and vibrant — much like a thriving market. Above, Anne had hung sprays of ferns from the beams along the length of the nave and, around the pulpit were beautiful golden roses.

'I say, Anne, it looks wonderful,' said James.

'You've worked so hard to make this a

celebration,' Beth added admiringly. 'I find the whole place inspiring.'

Anne flushed at the praise, explaining that she'd kept the roses in the fridge to keep them fresh. She excused herself to help the next villager in line. James steered Beth to the pews, where Charlie Hawkins pushed his children along to allow some room. Young Tommy Hawkins leant across his father.

'Me and Susan brought apples and some tins of tomato soup.'

Susan peeked over her brother. 'And a loaf of bread.'

'Splendid,' said James. 'You've certainly entered into the spirit of things.'

'Never mind that,' said Charlie to his children. 'You're supposed to be getting ready to sing. Go and sit with Mr Chrichton.'

They made their way along the pew and raced to the choir stalls.

James swung round to see the church filling up. Everyone, it seemed, had made a real effort. Graham Porter and his family waved from the opposite side. Messrs Chapman and Bateson, bank manager and solicitor respectively, sat alongside each other at the back. The Snoop Sisters, Rose and Lilac Crumb, whispered together, no doubt discussing their neighbours in rather negative terms. Dorothy Forbes and her husband slotted in immediately behind him and waved a hello.

Local farmers and their wives were, of course, the focus during harvest time and the villagers were keen to make room for them and treat them with much respect. Time spent away from their land and animals was normally time wasted, but they all took part in the harvest festivities and gave generously.

Donovan and Kate Delaney sat with their children between them. James suppressed a grin as Donovan squeezed a finger under his collar to loosen the restriction round his throat. Kate reached across and slapped his hand. He grimaced and tilted his chin out to alleviate the tightness.

Philip and Helen Jackson came down the aisle with their daughter, Natasha, and handed Anne a selection of fruit and vegetables. James squeezed up to allow them a seat.

'Thank you,' said Helen. 'What a wonderful turnout.'

'Isn't it?' James said as he saw Bert scurry down, hand Anne a bag of fruit and dash to a rear pew. Their cleaner, Mrs Jepson, followed him, nagging her husband to select a seat before they all went. The orchard grower, Pete Mitchell, shuffled to the rear of the church with his young wife.

Mr Bennett, James' boyhood fishing tutor, slowly walked toward Anne with a selection of wares from his allotment. His faithful dog, Blackie, ambled alongside him.

'Ow!'

The cry of anguish elicited a smile between James and Mr Chrichton, who had just clipped a young lad round the ear for misbehaving. The junior school choir were more used to school assemblies than formal church festivals and he felt Chrichton had his work cut out with this motley bunch, the bulk of the children being under twelve. They fidgeted, scratched and pushed one another until Chrichton drew himself up and quietly growled. The children stiffened. James tilted his head in wonder. He couldn't see Chrichton's face, but the growl certainly had the desired effect.

GJ and Catherine caught his eye as they waved. The stragglers, including George, skipped inside and took their places at the back.

Charlie leant close. 'Did you get your invite to Cory House?'

'Yes,' said James, 'Stephen called late last night.'

The call was unexpected but, he felt, a wonderful gesture. Calvin had insisted on an informal drinks party after the Harvest Festival for those villagers who had been so kind to Boyd.

Charlie whispered. 'Do you know who's been invited?'

'Just a handful of people,' said Beth 'Us, the Merryweathers, you, the Jacksons and DCI Lane.'

'DCI Lane?'

'Apparently they were impressed with his softly, softly approach to Boyd.'

A hush spread through the church. James turned to see Stephen leading Boyd, Calvin,

Suzie and Lucy down the aisle. After handing Anne their flowers and fruit, they took their places in the front pew that had been especially reserved for them. Before sitting they acknowledge James and Beth with a smile.

Stephen, who always preferred to be amongst his congregation rather than up in the pulpit, stood between the first pews and spread his arms open.

'Father God, we th-thank you for the gift of life and the abundance you provide; the flowers and fruits, the minerals and water, the living creatures and the g-grace and beauty of this land. At harvest time, the seeds we have sown reach their fruitfulness. Let us praise you for the harvest you supply each year.' He gave a nod to Mr Chrichton, who rapped the wooden rail between him and his pupils. They stood up. 'The ch-children of Cavendish Junior h-have rehearsed our most popular harvest hymn. P-please stand and join with them.'

And, as the congregation launched into 'We Plough the Fields and Scatter', so began the Harvest Festival service, a service that James particularly enjoyed because of its heritage and songs.

Stephen, as was his style, wandered up and down the aisle, engaging with villagers, weaving his biblical stories into riveting tales of lessons learnt, with the knack of gaining everyone's appreciation of the land and how precious the harvest was.

Bob Tanner stood to lead the first verse of 'Come, Ye Thankful People Come'. His voice was deep, rasping and mesmeric and the words and their meaning echoed through the church.

'Come, ye thankful people, come,
Raise the song of harvest home;
All is safely gathered in,
'ere the winter storms begin.
God our Maker doth provide,
For our wants to be supplied.
Come to God's own temple, come,
Raise the song of harvest home.'

The organ joined in during the second verse and the congregation was in full voice by the end. Stephen then invited James to speak. He slipped out of his seat.

Standing at the front, he smiled at the villagers and began his talk.

'When I was a small boy, my father made a point of taking me to see the farmers; to see how they toiled and worked the fields. I watched the heavy horses plough the land, vegetables planted, seeds sown and animals nurtured and cared for as if they were family. I stood in awe of the lone farmer trudging through snow to rescue his livestock. I felt humble, and continue to feel humble, when I'm among the farming community. Without them, we would not have the food we eat.' He unfolded a sheet of paper. 'I'm no singer, but I wanted to share a couple of verses of a song that many a farmer has sung since the last century. We hear it in the folk club and the pub and its words are particularly significant at this time of the year.'

He cleared his throat and recited the words:

'Let the wealthy and great roll in
    splendour and state,
I envy them not, I declare it.
For I eat my own ham, my own

chicken and lamb
I shear my own fleece and I wear it.

'By ploughing and sowing, by reap-
ing and mowing
King Nature affords me aplenty
I've a cellar well stored and a plenti-
ful board
And a garden affords every dainty.

'I have lawns, I have bowers, I have
fruit, I have flowers
And the lark is my morning alarmer
So jolly boys now here's good luck
to the plough
Long life and success to the farmer.'

The farmers were eager to show their
appreciation of James' speech and he gave
them a bashful smile as applause rippled
through the church. He took his place
next to Beth as Stephen continued.

'Before I end the harvest festivities and
move on to a short r-remembrance, I-I
would like to pass on something that I
recently heard a farmer saying on the
wireless.' He raised his voice and delivered

the quote with full conviction. 'We must look after the trees, the rivers, the oceans and the fields. When we lose sight of nature, it is then that we will realise that we have nothing. Man cannot live on money alone.'

A murmur went through the congregation and James sat back in full admiration of his friend. In a few words, he had highlighted how important the land was and refocused everyone's minds on the simple things in life. He returned his attention to Stephen, who was now standing in front of the Cameron family.

'As you know, the newcomers to our community, Christie and Jeannie Cameron, both suffered p-particularly unpleasant deaths. Their denomination, although different to ours, s-still upheld the love of God and the duty we have in serving our God. Christie's sons and nieces are here to join our community today in remembrance. Please b-bow your heads in prayer.'

As Stephen went through a selection of prayers, James' thoughts returned to the quote. So many lives lost or damaged in disputes over fortunes, property and possessions. The mysteries he'd been involved with so often had their root causes in greed. Would this be the same for the Camerons? Were the deaths of Christie and Jeannie to do with the vulgarity of money and inheritance? Or was Stephen right — was this something to do with the power of love?

Beth rested a hand on his shoulder. 'Come on, daydreamer. It's time to go.'

★　★　★

Cory House had taken on a brighter look of late. Work was still ongoing and there were more visible signs of a tired house coming to life. The ivy was now clear from the frontage and the stonework bright and clean. The weeds that had commandeered the gravel drive had been cleared. When the large front door opened, James was delighted by the warm welcome given to him and Beth; a far cry from the chilly reception on their first visit. What a breath of fresh air the nieces and the Cameron brothers were in comparison to Christie and his sister.

Lucy showed them into the front room

where the Jacksons and the Merryweathers were already tucking into cheese and pickle sandwiches. Luke and Mark Merryweather raced from room to room as Radley yelped and chased after them. Philip and Helen Jackson arrived with Natasha. Calvin, Lucy and Suzie buzzed back and forth from the kitchen with drinks and nibbles. Charlie sat cross-legged on the floor with his children, Tommy and Susan, getting them acquainted with Boyd, whose pink eyes were alive with anticipation.

Beth leant into James. 'What a shame Christie couldn't see Boyd as a wonderful human being.'

'Yes, I don't think there were any winners in that game,' replied James. 'At least Boyd can start living again.'

Suzie approached them with a jug and two glasses. 'Lucy made a non-alcoholic punch.' She screwed her face up in disgust. 'I don't see the point of it, really. It's only orange juice and lemonade. Why she couldn't put a bit of rum in there, I don't know.'

James accepted the glasses and watched as she filled them. 'It's a little early for rum punch, Suzie, and you're a little young to be drinking it.'

She pouted. 'I'm nearly sixteen.'

'Exactly.'

She turned on her heels and stomped off, much to their amusement. As Anne approached them, Beth asked James where George was.

'He made his excuses at the church and went back to the station.'

'Oh,' said Anne. 'Does that mean he's leaving you to investigate?'

She and Beth chuckled and James allowed them their fun. He scanned the room. 'Where's Stephen?'

'Outside. He was admiring the architecture so he's wandering around taking it all in.' She tutted. 'He was also intrigued by your searching for a secret passage.'

'Unfortunately, there isn't one — not as far as I could make out. Calvin looked, too.'

Anne shrugged and moved on to the subject of the harvest season. 'Well, those were our first scarecrow and Harvest Festivals in Cavendish and I've loved every minute of them. Are you all prepared for the supper?'

'Absolutely, old thing.' He'd already spoken with Graham Porter and the farmers about the food for the night and they'd decided on who would be supplying the geese, stuffing, gammon and vegetables. 'The junior school kitchen is supplying plates and cutlery and we're borrowing tables from the village hall.'

'How many are coming?'

Beth took over. 'Most of the villagers come, so we tend to seat the elderly first and the more able-bodied clamber onto the hay bales. James is Lord of the Harvest.'

Anne turned. 'I keep meaning to ask, but what does the Lord of the Harvest do?'

James explained that, traditionally, at the end of the harvest, farmers prepared a supper for those who helped bring the harvest home. Once the last of the corn was stored, the harvesters would elect a Lord of the Harvest.

'The Lord of the Harvest officially brings in the last sheaf of corn to

279

announce that the harvest is in. In Cavendish, we have this community supper. All of the farmers gather and everyone helps prepare the food. My job is to distribute harvest bread to everyone. Elsie Taylor's making loaves in the shape of a wheatsheaf. A caraway cake is also a traditional part of the meal.'

'And what's the significance of a caraway cake?'

'I believe that caraway seeds were symbolic of wheat grains,' said James. 'It appears to be a Sussex tradition so we've carried it on. It's normally eaten with ale, so Donovan is providing everyone with a tot of seasonal ale to accompany it.'

Anne had a satisfied smile on her face. 'I'm so pleased that Stephen is here as your vicar. It's lovely to be part of a village that keeps these traditions alive.'

James agreed and left the ladies to chat. He checked his watch. Stephen had been an awfully long time studying the outside of the house. What on earth had he found that was so interesting? He wandered through to the hall and down the front steps. The gravel crunched beneath his feet. He reached the corner and peered along the side.

'Oh my!' He dashed toward his friend, who was sitting against the wall with his head in his hands. 'Stephen, what's happened? Are you ill?'

Stephen slowly brought his head up and winced. 'Someone pushed me and I hit my head on the wall.'

James bent over Stephen and examined his head.

'You've got a nasty bruise coming up there. You may be concussed. Why don't I take you down to the hospital? It's only down the road.'

'Oh my goodness,' Anne said as she scurried to Stephen's side. 'What's happened?'

James, noting Stephen's subtle shake of the head, simply told her that her husband had tripped over. Beth joined them, wearing a concerned expression.

'What did you trip on?'

'F-fresh air, I'm afraid,' said Stephen.' I c-can be a little clumsy.' He closed his eyes. Out of earshot of the women, he whispered to James. 'I think it was that b-bulky chap from the f-festival. He was certainly a large man.'

'Are you sure?'

Stephen felt his head. 'As sure as I can be.'

After a brief examination by Philip Jackson, it was decided that a check-up would be the best thing. Philip insisted that Anne stay at Cory House and he would take Stephen himself. Ten minutes later, all had returned to normal and Anne chivvied Luke and Mark inside, insisting their father was not going to die. Beth sidled up to James who stood motionless, staring at the gravel.

'Penny for your thoughts?'

'He didn't trip over, Beth.'

'Oh my goodness!'

James went through the events as Stephen described.

'Do you think Locksmith Joe did this?' Beth asked.

'I really don't know what to think.'

'But yesterday evening you were convinced that this convict was innocent.'

Glancing beyond her, something caught his eye. He held her elbow lightly and guided her toward the back of the house.

'Where are we going?'

'Prying.'

At the rear of the garden was a substantial pile of junk seemingly ready for a bonfire. James picked up a sturdy stick and poked about.

Beth looked on. 'What on earth are you doing?'

'Searching for clues. Anne said some of the children from the village were rummaging around here. If Locksmith Joe was here, it would be for one reason only.'

'The camera!'

James rummaged around and picked out old clothes, discarded oil cans and a rusty kettle. He squatted down and picked up a small brown jar.

'What's that?' asked Beth.

He sniffed the contents and scrutinised the faded writing on the label. 'Some sort of glue.'

They frowned at each other. He threw the bottle back and poked about some more. There were old boots, a pile of moth-eaten overcoats and what appeared to be pieces of sheep's wool and bits of iron and wood. In truth, he knew that discovering the camera would be too good to be true. He picked up a hobnail boot and frowned.

'James, that's filthy, put it back.'

He examined it closely. The boots were familiar but he couldn't place them. James and Beth ambled back to the house.

'Sweetie, why would anyone want to harm Stephen?'

'I don't think there was any real intention. If it was Locksmith Joe, going by Bert's observations, he's not a violent man.' He wrapped an arm around Beth and they strolled back indoors where Calvin, Lucy and Suzie rushed to express their shock at the news.

'This bloody house is cursed,' said Calvin. 'The sooner we sell it the better.'

'Your father's probably haunting it,' said Lucy. 'He hated people and he probably hates everyone being here.'

'Well, he won't have to wait much longer for us all to clear out.'

★　★　★

Later that evening, James settled in front of the television to watch *Sunday Night at the London Palladium*. He snaked an arm around Beth's shoulders. Had Locksmith Joe been at the house to hunt for the camera? Who else could it have been? The telephone rang and James left Beth enjoying the programme to answer it.

'Hello James, it's Anne.'

'Anne, how's Stephen? Is he on the mend?'

'Slight concussion, that's all. They've kept him in overnight just to be on the safe side. He asked me to call you.'

'About?'

She whispered, 'He said he thinks he's seen where there could be a secret passage.'

James gasped. 'Really?'

'Yes, isn't it exciting? Anyway, he wondered if you could pick him up at the hospital tomorrow and he'll go through it with you.'

James expressed his thanks and returned to the lounge where Beth noted his expression.

'James, you look perplexed.'

'That was Anne. She says that Stephen

may have found a secret passage.'

'I thought you said there wasn't one? Had you better tell George?'

He slipped onto the sofa beside her.

'Not until I know for sure that it is one.' He faced Beth. 'Will you and Anne enter into a conspiracy, please? I need to make sure Cory House is empty.'

After some reluctance from Beth and a quick phone call, James organised a plan of action for the following day. He helped himself to a whisky and silently celebrated a possible breakthrough in the investigation of the deaths of Christie and Jeannie Cameron.

21

The matron at the cottage hospital on the outskirts of Cavendish pointed James in the direction of Stephen Merryweather. The reverend was dressed and sitting at the side of his bed with a cup of tea, staring out of the ward window.

'Ah Stephen, how are you?'

Stephen welcomed him with a smile. 'I'm qu-quite well, thank you and ready to go home. Shall I ask for another cup?'

'No, don't bother,' James unbuttoned his jacket and sat on the bed. 'Anne tells me you have an idea about a secret passage.'

'Yes.' Stephen put his tea down and pulled out a scrap of paper and a pen. 'I remember you talking about it the other day. I think I've seen an anomaly in the a-architecture. You only really see it if you step back.'

He pushed his teacup away and drew a sketch of the side wall. James shifted his position to observe.

'The b-building has two large chimneys on the left wall. They protrude so the wall isn't flat.'

He turned the drawing toward James. It was a crude and somewhat childish sketch but he didn't really see an anomaly. His friend smiled.

'Mm, I-I'm not Constable.' He discarded the drawing. 'But if you examine the wall from a distance, y-you will notice the left chimney is much wider than the right. And, if you stand a-against the wall, the left ch-chimney has more depth, too.'

★   ★   ★

Stephen met his gaze. 'You've seen the rooms. Is one fireplace bigger than the other?'

James stared out of the window and visualised the two rooms belonging to Boyd and Christie.

'No, not to warrant such an anomaly. Did you see any opening at all?'

'I s-saw some loose stonework. Th-that's when I was pushed.'

'Did this man come from the back of the house?'

'I think so. D-does that make a difference?'

James slid off the bed and helped
Stephen to his feet. 'Perhaps. You really
have to stop getting yourself knocked
about every time you look into something. Let's get you home, then I can go
and investigate.'

His friend pulled him back. 'You're
n-not going there alone, are you?'

James held Stephen's arm as they
wandered out. 'Absolutely not. Beth and
Anne have invited the Cameron brothers
and nieces to tea at Elsie's. Once they're
out of the way, Bert and I will visit Cory
House and see if we can find a way in.'

When he dropped Stephen off at the
vicarage, his friend poked his head back
through the open car window.

'D-do let me know how you get on.'

'I certainly will.' He put the Jaguar into
gear and sped off, quietly anticipating an
adventurous afternoon.

James parked the car in a lay-by a few
hundred yards from Cory House. He and
Bert scampered up the drive until they
arrived at the side wall of the impressive

building. He examined the structure and immediately saw what Stephen was driving at. Out of curiosity, he marched around the building to the opposite wall, where no such anomaly existed.

Returning to Bert, he saw his friend running his finger along the stonework.

'Anything?'

'Maybe. This line o' stones is narrower than the rest.'

James examined the ground and told Bert that the builders of the house had been expert masons. He drew attention to some of the intricate work that had gone into the construction. He squatted down, scooped up a powdery texture and rubbed it between his thumb and forefinger.

'Cement mix.'

Bert's probing fingers moved along the stonework and above the powder.

'Oi, oi. Look at this.' He eased out a loose stone and placed it on the ground. Bending over, he peered into the crevice and stood back to let James see.

James peered in. 'Good Lord!' He reached into the crevice and pulled a lever. A section of the wall pivoted inward to reveal a spiral, stone staircase.

They stood gawping at each other for several seconds before James spoke. 'Shall we?'

'It's what we're 'ere for,' said Bert. 'I'll follow you up.'

James reached into his pocket and brought out a small torch as he mounted the stairs. He likened them to the stone stairs he'd seen in large churches that led to the bell-tower. In a few seconds, they came to a narrow landing. He stopped one step below it. He felt Bert immediately behind him peering around his arm as he shone the torch about.

The beam picked out two further levers, one on either side of the landing.

'These must give access to the two bedrooms,' said James. 'This left one takes you through to Christie's room, the right one to Boyd's.'

He went to step up but Bert pulled him back.

'Shine yer light. There, on the top step.'

James shone the beam on the stone floor and frowned. Careful not to knock Bert back, he squatted down. Both sides showed a number of footprints in the dust.

'D'you see that?'

'Yeah. I reckon Boyd's been in and out a few times.'

'So have others, judging by the amount of activity in and out of Christie's room.'

'Yer gonna 'ave to tell George about this. Don't tread on the landing — he'll kill you if you mess that up.'

James handed Bert the torch and reached across to pull the left lever. As he did so, a gap appeared in the wall as part of it slid to the side. He stared at Bert, then reached across to the right lever and tried that. The wall opened a fraction of an inch but no more.

'I think something's blocking this.'

Bert nudged him to the left and, avoiding the top step, they ducked into Christie Cameron's bedroom. James gazed at the opening and studied it with a sense of wonder. Whoever designed this had made a jolly fine job of camouflaging it. Bert began opening drawers, feeling under shelves and checking the top of the wardrobe.

'What're you doing?'

'Seeing if there's a camera or film 'ere.'

'I say, was Locksmith Joe here yester-day?'

Bert shrugged and said he hadn't seen him for a couple of days. 'Why?'

'I'll go through it with you later,' replied James. 'Meanwhile, let's see if we can find that camera and anything else that may give us a clue.' He checked his watch. They still had a while. 'You check here. I'll check the other rooms. Be careful to put everything back as you find it. Should we wear gloves or something?'

Bert told him to use his handkerchief if he was going to pick about. He made his way out onto the landing and across to Jeannie Cameron's room. Like Christie's, it was sparse and held nothing in the way of a memento or souvenirs. But, to be thorough, James left no stone unturned and rummaged through every drawer, cupboard and shelf in sight. He heaved himself inside the loft through a trapdoor in the ceiling, but his torchlight picked out nothing but cobwebs and dust.

His last port of call was Boyd's room, which was a mass of books, photographs, toys and models. He stood in the doorway. A sense of guilt fell on him. Bert came out of the spare room to join him.

'What's up? Whatcha waiting for?'

'I can't search Boyd's things. It's not right.'

Bert rested a hand on his shoulder. 'Would this Christie bloke 'ave stashed it with his boy?'

'I wouldn't have thought so. Boyd's too inquisitive. If he found a film, I would hazard a guess that he'd try to develop it.'

He felt Bert tap his shoulder lightly. 'Then we leave it. There's nothin' up 'ere. Let's try downstairs.'

James held an index finger up as a reminder and dashed over to the secret doorway that was still ajar.

'Here. Boyd must have moved this bookcase out of the way when he went out. This must be how he escaped to the scarecrow festival.' He checked his watch again. 'We've been some time. I asked Beth to keep them away for at least an hour.'

'Will she stall 'em?'

'I've no idea,' replied James. 'They may have plans or something. Bert, I really don't want to be found creeping around here. We can perhaps check downstairs another time.'

However, Bert nudged him forward and, before he had a chance to protest, he found himself standing in the hallway.

'Right, Jimmy boy, you take the front room, I'll do the kitchen.'

James went through to the room he'd first entered on his initial visit to Cory House. What a different place it was now. Boyd's books and models were scattered across the table tops and floor, a couple of photos were perched on the mantelpiece and the religious tapestries and crosses had been replaced by landscape pictures.

There was little furniture, however, so searching drawers and cupboards took him only a couple of minutes. Bert appeared in the doorway.

'Anything?'

'Nothing,' said James. With a start, he looked up.

Gravel crunched outside.

He froze.

His heart thumped.

They dashed into the hall and bounded up the stairs. On the landing, James glimpsed over the banister in time to see an envelope flutter onto the door mat.

He closed his eyes in relief. 'It's the ruddy postman.'

Bert grinned and pushed him into Christie's room and back through the walled doorway.

James looked down to check his footing and something caught his eye. 'Bert, what's that? There, by your left foot?'

His friend bent down and picked up a slip of paper and handed it to James, who slipped it into his pocket.

'I'll look at that later. Let's get out of here before they get back.'

Inside the passageway James pulled the lever and watched the secret door close. He reached to the right and did the same to close the door on Boyd's room.

He squinted as they emerged into the sunlight. Another pull of a lever and the walled door shut tight — a perfect join.

Bert replaced the loose stone. 'That's a right clever bit o' work, ain't it? Proper mason work. I 'eard they often slipped in a secret passage and now we've seen one.'

'Ingenious,' replied James. 'Come on. I'm really not comfortable being here, they could be back at any minute.'

They flitted through the trees and shrubs that lined the driveway. James' heart beat a little slower once they'd got off the property and to the car unseen. He chivvied Bert along and couldn't relax until he'd driven some distance from the house, where he eventually pulled onto a grass verge and they both lit a cigarette.

'Bert, I can't thank you enough for coming. You provide me with a sense of confidence in such situations.'

'You've always 'elped me, Jimmy boy. And, let's face it, this is more my line than yours.'

'Do you want dropping off somewhere?'

After delivering Bert to the bus stop, James returned home. Beth was still out, so he went to telephone George. Before he could do so, however, the telephone rang. He grabbed the receiver.

'Cavendish 261?'

'Sweetie, it's me.'

'Oh, hello darling. I thought you'd be back.'

'I won't be long, but I thought you'd want to know. That man you met at the Wendover.'

'Swiss?'

'That's him. He called just as you left earlier. He wants us to meet him for dinner tonight. I didn't know if you had plans so I said you'd call him. I've left the number on the pad by the phone. I'm happy to go if you are.'

James read the message. 'Did he have a reason for wanting to see us?'

'Only that he hinted that he had some information that you may find interesting?'

'Right-ho. I'll give him a call now.'

'How did you get on?'

'Are you still with the Camerons?'

'We're about to drop them home now.'

James indicated that his excursion with Bert was a waste of time and hung up. While Beth could easily keep this to herself, he didn't want to instil any excitement in her, especially with Anne about, who could sniff out a clue at the drop of a hat. No, he'd update Beth on the way to London.

Good. Things were coming together. They'd discovered a way into the locked room and now Swiss might have some vital information. He dashed upstairs with the excitement of a schoolboy receiving a new Meccano set.

22

At Haywards Heath railway station, James purchased two return tickets to Victoria and, turning, collided with George.

'George! What're you doing here?'

'I called the house and Mrs Jepson was there. Said you were off to London, so I took a chance that you'd be here.' He pulled them away from the ticket desk. 'I understand Stephen was attacked.'

James checked the huge station clock. The train was due in ten minutes. He relayed a bite-sized version of what had occurred at Cory House and, to Beth's astonishment, he revealed the secret of the locked room. George tensed and James knew he'd overstepped the mark.

'I'm sorry, George. I know I should have called to let you know. I was about to do that earlier but then I received a message to see Swiss.'

An announcement interrupted them. The train was imminent.

'George, I promise to call you first thing tomorrow and I can show you how it all works.'

George pulled him round to face him. 'No. What you'll do, the pair of you, is come down to the station in the morning. I'm going to need this in a statement.'

The train eased into the station and came to a halt. James opened the door of the First Class carriage for Beth. George, showing his credentials, had followed them onto the platform.

'I say, George, this Locksmith Joe chap. Was it a cut and dried case, him being a killer and all?'

His friend frowned. 'Why're you asking?'

James shut the door behind him and slid the window down. 'Oh, no reason. Just curious.'

As the train moved off, he heard George call out. 'If you know something, James . . . '

James waved, slid the window shut and sat down next to Beth, who pushed him for details about the secret passage. He stood up, took his overcoat off and told her. From the anomalies in the architecture that Stephen had seen, to the loose stonework, the spiral staircase and the footprints on the top step. He described their search for the missing camera and film and his feeling that it had probably been destroyed long ago.

'It's the one piece of evidence that incriminates Christie, so why would he keep it?'

'For the reason that you said,' replied Beth. 'Perhaps he felt guilty. But why do any of us keep things that may provoke a bad memory? I still have a photograph of me and my father after we'd had an awful row and we both look as if we're eating lemons. Every time I look at it, I think of that row and how we'd spoken to each other. I can't even remember what we argued about. Why I don't throw it away, I don't know.'

'Then why not give himself up and allow an innocent man to go free?'

'Because he's a coward.'

'That word's come up a couple of times now. We didn't know Christie, but he gave us the impression he was a figurehead of the family, an upright citizen, strict Presbyterian and all. But all this bluster and anger, his treatment of his wife and sons. Those are not the actions of a man in control.'

'Those, sweetie, are the actions of a bully.'

'And underneath it all, a bully is simply a coward; someone who can't face up to his own failings, so picks on others to boost his own ego.' James held a finger up as if to emphasise the point. 'Locksmith Joe claims he saw Christie kill his wife before placing the blame on him. He has two wonderful sons that he sees as imperfect and lays the blame on his wife. He moves here to Cavendish and, from what I can see, treated his sister with as much contempt as he did the rest of us.'

'Is this getting you to some sort of conclusion?' asked Beth.

'I wish to goodness it was,' said James with a hint of exasperation. 'I keep talking everything through, hoping that something may make sense.'

Beth suggested he get back to basics. 'Who are your suspects? If you're discounting Locksmith Joe, you have four: Boyd, Calvin, Lucy and Suzie. You are going to have to admit that one of them is a killer. And one of them attacked Stephen. We can't be sure that Boyd isn't involved, especially if he knew about the passage.'

'But Stephen is sure that it was Locksmith who pushed him. And the other suspects are nowhere near the same build and wouldn't have had time to disguise themselves.'

She gave him an old-fashioned look. 'You have to make your mind up whether to believe Joe's story or not. It sounds to me like you have doubts.'

He held Beth's hand. 'Let's see what Swiss has to say. He wouldn't ask us all the way up here without good reason.'

☆ ☆ ☆

Graves led them through the smoky reception area of the Wendover to an intimate restaurant in an enclosed courtyard at the back of the club. Swiss rose from his chair, took James' hand and gave a gracious welcome to Beth, who commented on the ambience once they were seated.

'Yes, it's nice, isn't it?' replied Swiss. 'You probably remember this as a place to sit during the summer, James. They put a roof on it a few months ago, so we can come out here all year round.'

It was a typical cobble stoned courtyard, with plants in large pots strategically placed to provide privacy for the diners. The roof above them consisted of a number of glass skylights, allowing a good deal of sunlight in during the day. This evening, the canopy above was of the constellations.

James counted twelve wrought iron tables, each with four heavy iron chairs with thick cushions for comfort. The waiter distributed a menu listing snacks and dinner items.

During the next hour, they enjoyed a light fish supper, caught up with news about members, Swiss's work events, Harrington's country hotel, their respective families and recent holidays and exploits.

Over coffee, James swirled his brandy in a bowl glass and met Swiss's gaze. 'This has all been rather lovely, but I believe it's time we moved on to why we're really here.'

Swiss flicked ash from his cigar onto the small glass ashtray beside him. 'You got me thinking about the Cameron family when we last met. He came up in conversation earlier today with a mutual colleague; the one I told you about, Quinn, the man who used to help with Cameron's investments more than I did — his financial advisor, so to speak. Anyway, I got to talking to him and asked how well he knew Christie Cameron.'

'And?'

'He knew him better than I did. I'll go through his thoughts with you. They may be of some help or I may be wittering on about nothing, but it's actually quite a dramatic story.'

James continued swirling his brandy but felt his heart skip a beat. Swiss sipped his liqueur.

'Quinn actually went to Yorkshire to discuss finances with him. He was up that way for our company one time and he suggested he call in to save Cameron making the journey down here.'

'This is Cameron's place in Otley?'

'Yes, just outside. Quite settled there, as far I know. That's why I thought it odd that he moved to Cavendish.' Swiss shifted forward. 'Well, that's the first thing I must tell you. That house in Cavendish was his. He purchased it years ago.'

'I say, really?'

'It belonged to the Cory family, is that right?'

Both James and Beth answered at the same time. 'Yes.'

'Well, there was one branch of family related to the Corys and guess whose that was?'

'Christie Cameron?'

Swiss nodded. 'The Cory family died out and the Camerons were the only connection to that side of the family. Christie's wife wanted to live in the house. It was near her family and she begged him to move. She thought it was a wonderful family home. He refused to move, wanted nothing to do with it — until moving in a few weeks ago.'

He took a sip of his drink.

'Well, I remember Quinn coming into the office after his visit and he was in a reflective mood, for want of a better word.'

'Reflective?'

Swiss gave them a smile. 'It's not like Quinn to be reflective. He's rather gregarious and intense in the office, so when he arrived without much to say, it caught my attention. But he wouldn't speak of his visit — not one bit of it.'

A short silence followed as if Swiss was thinking of how to continue. 'Well, today, I tackled him about it. He didn't want to say anything at first, but once I told him that Christie and his sister were dead . . . well, it was as if a weight had lifted. He told me that he'd been glad to get out of that house; that the whole family were bonkers.'

James and Beth were lost for words.

Swiss continued. 'He'd arrived that afternoon and Cameron blasted him for being early. He was only ten minutes early, but he wouldn't let him in for five minutes.'

'Why on earth not?'

'Shouted at someone, his sister I presume, something about hiding it, or him, or something. Then Quinn heard footsteps running up the stairs. Then Cameron opened the door and let him in.' His brow knitted together. 'Isn't that a little odd?'

James said that it wasn't and Beth let Swiss know about Boyd and the Camerons' shame at having an albino in the family.

Swiss listened with increasing horror. 'Good grief. The poor lad could have only been a toddler. Can you imagine being discriminated against by your own father?'

'Did he notice anything else?' asked James.

'Lord, yes.' Swiss explained how Quinn had gone to sit down on a chair in the living room and was ordered to sit anywhere but there. 'He reacted similarly in the kitchen, apparently. All the chairs were the same, but Cameron insisted he avoid one chair in particular.' He lowered his voice. 'Then he did something.'

James and Beth waited in anticipation.

'He said something like *I've had enough of this torment*. Then he picked

309

up the offending chair, opened the kitchen door and threw it outside.'

'Oh my goodness,' said Beth.

'Not only that,' continued Swiss. 'He picked up an axe and chopped it into pieces.'

Beth dragged her chair closer. 'Then what?'

'Then his eldest son came down and . . . '

They waited patiently. James observed Swiss. It was as if he were trying to comprehend what he was saying.

'His eldest son, Calvin, picked up a carving knife. He could've only been thirteen or fourteen. He picked up the knife and screamed at his father to stop it. He just kept repeating that over and over. *Stop it, stop it, stop it.*' Swiss rolled his eyes. 'You can imagine how Quinn was feeling at this point. He went to interrupt, but Cameron stormed back in the kitchen, grabbed the knife from his son and plunged it into the boy's thigh.'

Beth brought her hands to her mouth. 'Oh, dear God.'

'The sister came down and shouted at Quinn to get out. When he got outside,

Cameron threatened him. *You say a word about any of this and you're a dead man. That's what he said.*' Swiss puffed his cheeks. 'It's a wonder Calvin didn't bleed to death.'

As the waiter cleared the table, the three of them sat in stunned silence. James processed the information in his head and wondered if any of this, although interesting, had given any semblance of order to things. It certainly proved one thing. He was quite sure that Christie Cameron was capable of murder.

If Locksmith Joe could prove his innocence, that left him with Boyd, Calvin, Lucy and Suzie as his main suspects.

*   *   *

The clickety-clack of the train lulled him into a daze as he watched the lights of London twinkle and fade into the distance. Beth rested her head on his shoulder.

'It has to be Calvin,' she said, sitting upright. 'Calvin has the most reason to kill.'

'But that knife incident happened years

ago. Why come all the way from India to kill him now? And he wasn't in the country when Christie was killed.' James sat up with a start and felt his pocket. 'Damn. I'd forgotten all about this.'

'About what?'

He used his handkerchief to bring out a slip of paper and waved it in triumph. 'This. I found it in the secret stairway.'

He unfolded it. It was part of a letter, but he only had one page of it. It held neither an address nor a signature. It was written in blue ink in a considered hand. Beth linked an arm through his and asked him to read it aloud. He cleared his throat.

' . . . *shadow has cast itself upon us. That abominable man wants to come between us but we won't let it. You know we can't let it. Love is too powerful to be defeated. I will do anything and I will for that love to . . .* '

James waved the paper. 'That's it.'

'Are you sure there were no more pieces there?'

'We didn't see any, no.'

Beth sat up and faced him. 'This is

clearly a love letter. The emotion there is heartbreaking. It sounds like two people who have had to live apart and are determined to be together.' She grabbed his arm. 'That's not Calvin's handwriting, is it?'

'I'm sure it isn't. His is a little more scrawled than this.' James rested his back on the cushioned seat then sat up straight. 'This takes me back to when Calvin turned up at Cory House.'

'When Lucy arrived?'

'Yes. The more I think about it, the more I believe that she is in love with him. There was a radiance about her. She checked her hair and smoothed her dress down.'

'As if she was meeting someone special.'

'Yes.' James thought for a moment. 'We need to get her to write something — then we can check it against this.'

'So, she's in love with Calvin,' said Beth, 'who may or may not be married.'

'Ye . . . es,' replied James, with little conviction.

'But they're first cousins!'

'Yes, that makes it rather worrying.'

The train pulled into Haywards Heath and they alighted. As they made their way to the exit, James stopped and stared at a theatre poster. Beth followed his gaze and read the announcement.

'*Leave It to Jane*, performed by the Haywards Heath amateur dramatic society.' She inclined her head quizzically. 'Do you want to see this?'

James grabbed her hand. 'No. I want to read through those letters again.'

Much to Beth's alarm, James put his racing head on and sped the Jaguar home from the station. He dismissed the idea of parking the car in the garage and dashed up the steps to the front door. Beth scurried behind him.

'Will you tell me what you're hoping to find?'

He threw his keys on the table, winked at her and strode through to the lounge. Beth flicked the lights on as he retrieved the shoebox. Rummaging through the envelopes, he pulled one letter out, then another, then another. Some he put to one side, some he replaced. After several minutes, a familiar sense of achievement came over him.

'Darling, come and have a look at this.' Beth joined him on the sofa. 'These handwritten letters all refer to Calvin's lady friend and bride, or alleged bride. He refers to her as Jayne. J-A-Y-N-E. When we switch to the two typed letters we have, she is referred to as Jane. J-A-N-E.'

She fixed her gaze on the letters. 'You don't spell your wife's name wrong.'

'Either he dictated this letter, or someone else wrote this.'

'Oh my goodness. Are you saying Calvin isn't Calvin?'

James leapt up and grabbed a whisky bottle and two glasses. 'I've absolutely no idea. But if you are enclosing a photograph of your wife at her wedding, wouldn't you send one of the pair of you? And, if Calvin is not Calvin, then who is he?'

'And if Calvin isn't Calvin, how come everyone recognises him?'

James poured them both a glass of twelve-year-old malt. 'I'm telephoning George.'

After imparting the news about the

knife attack and the letters, George reiterated his instructions.

'James. Come in first thing, you and Beth, to make some official statements. I'm playing this low-key. If that's not Calvin, who is it? And if it's not Calvin, he's dangerous and ruddy clever. Let's let him think we accept him for who he is. So, if you see him, act normal. I'll get on to the hospitals in Yorkshire — see if we can't get that attack on him confirmed. If it was that bad, he must have had some treatment. I want the full facts before I go barging in. And bring those letters. I'm beginning to think the whole blooming family is involved.'

With arrangements complete, James returned to the lounge where Beth thrust the photographs at him; small black and white prints that Calvin had sent to Boyd over the years. She stabbed the images with her finger.

'Why didn't we see this before, James? See how alike they are. Boyd and the girls haven't seen Calvin in ten years. Calvin and Josh have the same hair, eyes, the same height and build, and are both from the same area. They're practically brothers and look similar too. And they've known everything about each other since childhood.'

'You're absolutely right, Beth. Josh has taken Calvin's place. I don't know how I'm going to sleep with all of this in my head.'

Beth grabbed a pad. 'Well, let's write it down so we don't forget anything for George.'

He checked the mantel clock. Ten o'clock. It would be a long night, he knew, but at last they had had some sort of breakthrough.

23

James and Beth signed their respective statements and thanked a young woman police constable for their teas.

George, sitting behind a desk strewn with papers and folders, prepared his pipe.

'I haven't checked that secret passage yet. I'm waiting till everyone's out of the house. I'm mindful of keeping things on an even keel; don't want to alert Calvin of any suspicion. There's a constable hovering nearby to tell me when the coast is clear. But from what you've said, I think Boyd went to the scarecrow festival via the secret passageway.'

'That's my thinking, too,' said James.

'I want to believe that the same person is responsible for both murders,' continued George.

'But then it can't be Calvin or Josh, or whoever. He didn't get here until after Christie's death.'

'Oh George,' said Beth, 'you certainly have your work cut out.'

George let out a frustrated *pah!* 'On a positive note, I managed to speak to the nurse that treated Calvin and I think I know why the Camerons moved.'

'Really?' said James.

'Christie Cameron had been going to the doctor on and off since his wife was killed. Apparently, he'd slowly lost weight and, although he was always a religious man, he became more so after her death, obsessively so. The police had a couple of reports of strange behaviour. The reports they filed describe a man on the edge, mentally. He was an angry man at the best of times, but even more after Gwen died.'

Beth sat forward. 'That makes sense. Swiss said that, when his colleague went to sit down on specific chairs, Christie screamed at him. I'll bet you they were the chairs Gwen used. I mean, most people sit in the same place, don't they?'

'So,' added James, 'he's cut up about his wife's death. Being eaten up from the inside by the sounds of it. He ups sticks

319

to Cavendish to live in the house his wife begged him to move to when she was alive. It's as if he's trying to make it up to her.'

George grunted that this was how he saw it. 'Poor bloke. We all put him down for being a stubborn old man, but there was a reason behind some of that behaviour.'

James gritted his teeth. How he wished he could let George know about Locksmith Joe. It was clear that Christie was been so riddled with guilt he was slowly destroying himself, while trying to make amends. Unfortunately, he went about it the wrong way. He drummed his fingers on the desk.

'What about the nurse?'

'She was a trainee back then, but she remembered the incident because she didn't believe the story they gave.' George pushed tobacco into the pipe bowl. 'Christie made up some story about playing with knives. She was intimidated by him and he threatened her before they left.'

'Threatened her?'

George went on to tell how Christie threatened to harm those she loved if she ever thought about reporting it.

'If it happened now, she said she would have called the police straight away. But she was young, still training and didn't want to make a scene.'

He lit the pipe. 'It was a deep gash, needed a few stitches. She told them that he should keep coming back to have dressings changed and make sure it was kept clean, but she never saw them again.'

'So, there'd be a scar?' asked James.

'Yes, and it damaged some muscle. The nurse said she'd be surprised if there wasn't a slight limp.' George dragged his chair forward and put his elbows on the desk. 'Right, at least I have something tangible. When I confront the alleged Calvin, I can insist on seeing the scar. That'll prove this theory beyond reasonable doubt.'

'Unfortunately,' said James, 'it doesn't prove he's a murderer, just that he's assumed another identity.'

'And where is the real Calvin?' asked George. 'Your chap Kushal seemed to think he'd booked passage. I'll need to check Calvin's passport.'

'Haven't you done that?'

'Unfortunately not,' replied George. 'And I'm sure my superior won't let me forget it.'

James held up a finger. 'Well, fortunately for you, I am a little ahead. Both Kushal and my contact at Somerset House, Gerald Crabtree, have contacts in Bombay.'

Gerald Crabtree had proved to be a useful acquaintance since their meeting in the spring. His access to family archives was invaluable. 'I made a point of contacting them yesterday.' He checked his watch. 'Shall I telephone and see if they've found anything out?'

George pushed the phone toward him. James' first port of call was Gerald Crabtree. On learning that James was with the police, Gerald dispensed with the pleasantries and went straight to the facts.

'My counterpart at the records office has checked and double-checked marriages and deaths over the last two years.

Obviously, there have been a number but he can't find anything under the name of Cameron. Would he have used a pseudonym?'

'I doubt it,' said James. 'If anything, he'd want that name on the certificate to please his father.'

'In that case, I'm not sure that I can be of any help.'

James hid his disappointment and thanked Gerald. After imparting the news to Beth and George, he dialled Kushal's number.

'Ah, James, you are the person I was just thinking of calling.'

'Splendid, I'm with George at the moment. Do you have any news?'

'Calvin Cameron is still in Bombay.'

James almost dropped the receiver. 'Still in Bombay . . . ?' Beth and George stared at him. 'Oh Lord . . . When did this happen?' James mimed holding an invisible pen at George who thrust a pencil into his hand. He scribbled down 'May.' 'And the prognosis?' He scribbled some more.

'This is of some help to you, James?'

'Most informative, Kushal. Thank you so much. I'll be in touch.' James replaced the receiver slowly. Beth pushed him to speak up.

'Calvin Cameron is in a hospital in Bombay. He was struck down by a mysterious illness. He's been in and out of hospital since May. However, for the last month, he's been confined to his bed. They're concerned about the long-term prognosis. The doctors have hinted that he may lose his life.'

'Oh no,' said Beth.

George remained silent. James studied the pad.

'May, this year,' continued James thoughtfully. 'That's when he was admitted to hospital. That coincides with the letters changing from handwritten to type. I believe Josh took over corresponding with Boyd. He knew how much Boyd meant to Calvin so he continued writing.' He looked at George. 'That's what changed. That's why Calvin wanted Boyd over there — to see him before he dies.'

James slammed the desk with his hand and brought out the slip of paper he'd found on the stairwell. ' . . . *shadow has cast itself upon us. That abominable man wants to come between us but we won't let it. You know we can't let it. Love is too powerful to be defeated. I will do anything and I will for that love to . . .* '

He threw the paper down. 'This isn't a letter from Lucy. This is from Josh to Calvin. This is the inappropriate affair. The forbidden love that so sickened Christie.'

24

After stopping for tea in Lewes, they took a slow drive back to Cavendish. Beth suggested they call in at the vicarage.

'Good idea. We can see how Stephen is faring after his attack.' As they entered Cavendish, James sped past the vicarage and parked outside the library.

'Why have you stopped here?' asked Beth.

'I want to check the airline timetables to see if they match what Calvin said.'

The library, a converted terraced cottage, gave off the delightful musty smell of books and buzzed with activity. Mr Chrichton had brought one of his classes over and the excited children were picking out books from the junior section to take back to school. Charlie left the boys and girls to it and welcomed James and Beth.

'What brings you here?'

'I wondered if we could take a look at

the timetables you have for the airlines?'

Charlie told them to follow him up the stairs to a small reference section. One shelf was full of bus, train and airline timetables, along with ferry and tide information. He pulled out two books and put them on a small desk.

'This covers the global network. You thinking of going away?'

'I wish we were,' said Beth, who added that James wanted to check Calvin's itinerary.

'Good luck with that. It's a real trek from India to England. I bet he had to change a few times, too.'

James agreed. 'Do you have a pen and paper?'

'In the table drawer. Help yourself. I'd best get downstairs and stamp some of these books out for the kiddies.'

Charlie left them to it and James and Beth sat down on two wobbly wooden chairs.

'I say, do you have the itinerary George gave you?' said James.

Beth reached into her handbag and brought out a sheet of paper. She unfolded it and placed it on the table.

'The first flight he took was from Bombay to Delhi on 19th September departing at 09:45.'

James flicked through the flimsy pages and examined the small print. He pressed his index finger to the schedules column and slowly followed it down.

'Here we are, Bombay to Delhi — nine forty-five. Where next?'

'Delhi to Beirut. That left at two in the afternoon.'

He flicked through the pages again and found the desired column. Scanning the entries, he saw that the flight did exist. Beth read out the next flight.

'Beirut to Paris. That left the following day at eleven-thirty in the morning.'

James checked again. 'Yes, that one's there too.' He slammed the timetable shut. Beth frowned.

'This is a fruitless exercise, Beth. Our man Calvin — or, rather, Josh — is not a stupid man. The information he's given to George will check out. The only way he could have been in the country to murder Christie is if he changed his flight.'

'But wouldn't George have checked his travel arrangements?'

'I'm certain that Josh killed Cameron. George's people checked his travel, but I wonder if they slipped up?'

'But how?' asked Beth. 'He can't have travelled on an earlier flight and then checked in for one a few days later. That's impossible.'

James scratched his head. Something was nagging at him and he wished to goodness it would produce an idea. He knew there was an answer to this, but it shied away from his conscious thinking.

They heard Charlie trot back up the stairs. 'Everything all right?'

James returned the books to the shelf. 'Yes, fine thanks. I need to make a call. Is there a telephone in the library?'

'Closest one is the phone box on the corner.'

'Not to worry, we're just off to the Merryweathers. I'll call in a favour from him. Come along, darling.'

Five minutes later, Anne ushered them into their front room and she and Beth went to the kitchen to prepare coffee and cake. James sat on the armchair opposite Stephen and asked after his health.

'Full recovery, th-thank you.' Stephen reached across, picked up a folded sheet of paper and handed it to James, who flicked it open.

'*Dear Rev, Sorry I hurt you. I thought the house would be empty for a bit. Hope you are all right. Joe.*'

James couldn't help but smile. Bert's description of Locksmith Joe's character was spot on. He wouldn't hurt a fly and just knowing he'd pushed Stephen a little too hard had prompted a written apology.

'Y-you really believe him to be innocent?' asked Stephen.

'Most certainly,' replied James. Radley, the springer spaniel, leapt on him. 'Ah, hello young Radley.' He fondled the dog's ears. 'They are incredibly affectionate, aren't they? I wouldn't mind a little pooch myself, to be honest.

'I say, would you mind if I used your telephone? I have a contact at BOAC and I believe he may be able to help me.'

Stephen said he should do whatever was necessary. As he got to the hall, Anne peered round the kitchen door.

'Oh gosh, is this to do with your investigation?'

He smiled at her. She really did relish a mystery. Beth joined her as he picked up the receiver and placed some coins by the phone for the call.

'I wondered if Ronnie Pickering was in his office,' he said to Beth. 'He may be able to find out a little more about these flights. You carry on and I'll join you in a few minutes.'

They went through to the front room as James placed his call. Five minutes later he returned, rubbing his hands.

Anne was the first to react. 'Goodness, have you found something out?'

'Not yet, but Ronnie has a number of contacts in the industry. I've left dates and names with him and he's going to get back to me. They need to check back on passenger lists for Calvin and Josh.'

'W-why are y-you interested in J-Josh?' asked Stephen.

James almost choked on his coffee. 'You don't know, do you?' He and Beth spent the next thirty minutes telling them the news about Calvin and Josh and the altercation between Christie and Locksmith Joe.

Their friends sat in silence and, from their open-mouthed expressions, it was clear they found it difficult to process the information. The questions then came thick and fast and both James and Beth did their best to answer them. Stephen expressed his shock over the revelation of Locksmith Joe.

'And you b-believe him?'

'Absolutely, especially after the story Swiss told us. Christie Cameron seemed to be a somewhat volatile man and became more so after his wife was killed. He showed the classic signs of a man racked with guilt.'

'A-and to stab your own s-son . . . ' Stephen deliberated on this for a moment. 'And you think that Christie Cameron may have held onto the camera?'

James shrugged. 'I honestly don't know. However, judging by his behaviour since his wife's death, I'd say it's hidden somewhere. Bert and I did our best to search the house but we couldn't find anything. And it wasn't hard — there's hardly anything there.'

Anne shuddered. 'The boys were sneaking around the Cory House grounds last week and said there was a rubbish tip at the back.'

'Yes,' James said. 'I saw that after we discovered Stephen. There was quite a lot of junk there — old clothes, shoes and oil cans.'

'Sweetie,' said Beth, 'if the clothes were old, they obviously brought those with them, so there's still hope that the camera may be there.'

'U-unless it all b-belonged to the previous owner?' put in Stephen.

'I guess. That's where they found Boyd's scarecrow outfit.'

James clicked his thumb and finger. 'Of course! It's just dawned on me what that glue was that I found in that rubbish tip.' He met Beth's eyes. 'Spirit glue.'

'The theatrical glue? For the moustache and sideburns?'

'Yes.' He sat forward. 'And those hobnail boots. I thought I'd seen them before because there are so many scuff marks on them. I'm sure, if we look at those photographs George had developed, we'll see our suspect dressed up in those old clothes and boots. He would have used sheep's wool to resemble a beard. There were plenty of overcoats on that pile of rubble. He only had to put a couple on and he would immediately take on the appearance of a larger man.'

'If that's what happened, then Josh is our murderer,' said Anne.

James was quick to argue the point. 'What about Lucy? She's as tall as Josh. She had opportunity and motive. She benefits from the will.'

'And not o-one person recognises Josh?'

'The last time anyone saw Calvin, he would have been around fifteen — ten years have gone by. He and Josh have gone from scrawny boys to strapping men. That's an awfully long time to hold on to an image.'

'And,' Beth put in, 'if you study the few photographs of Calvin and Josh in Bombay, they're remarkably similar in build and expression. They could easily pass themselves off as brothers.'

'The photographs are quite grainy,' continued James. 'Boyd and the girls have assumed Josh is Calvin. They have no reason to believe otherwise.'

Beth reminded everyone that Josh would have known Boyd. 'After all, he and Calvin were great friends at school, so it's not as if he had to memorise anything.'

Stephen rested back in his chair. Radley hopped up and nestled next to Anne, who suddenly sat up straight.

'What are you going to do? Confront him?'

'George is going across to speak with him,' replied James. 'But I'm sure he'll have a reason for taking on Calvin's identity and it won't include murder. We simply have no proof. It's all hypothetical. I'm not sure that you can charge someone with impersonation.' He turned to Beth. 'I can't sit here pondering. I have to try something else. Shall we have a word with Lucy? Do you think she knows more than she's letting on?'

'Won't she be at work?'

'Even better. I'd rather not have Josh in the vicinity, if truth be told.'

'But what if she's in on it?' asked Anne.

'Well, she's not going to do anything in an office,' replied James. 'If she does admit to murder, we'll keep her there and call the police.'

After finishing their coffee and cake, James and Beth began their journey to Hove.

25

Alliance Insurance was situated two streets back from the seaside promenade in Hove. The typing pool consisted of approximately thirty women frantically striking the keys for their respective managers and directors. The noise deafened James as he and Beth followed the office manager, Mr Smythe, into the area. Smythe scanned the pool and held a finger up in recognition. He asked that James and Beth remain where they were. He strode to the middle of the room where Lucy Braithwaite was typing furiously. Beth sidled up to James.

'It's a wonder these women can hear themselves think in here.'

James agreed as Lucy waved to them. She gathered her things and followed Smythe as he walked toward them.

'Lord Harrington, Lady Harrington. What a surprise.'

She seemed flustered, avoided eye

contact and secured a stray wisp of hair behind her ear. Smythe led them along a corridor and into his office. He checked his watch.

'I've a few errands to run so you can have this place for half an hour. Do you want a drink? The tea lady's due to come round in a while.'

They declined. Smythe pulled the door to and James arranged three chairs in a circle and asked Lucy to join them. She sat down and bit her lip.

'Is everything all right?' she asked anxiously. 'Has someone been arrested? Have they picked up Locksmith Joe? He did it, didn't he?'

James glanced at Beth, who was equally surprised at the accusation, then returned his attention to Lucy.

'Why would you think that, Lucy?'

Her eyes darted between the pair of them. 'Well, isn't it obvious? He's in the area. He's come back to kill everyone else.'

'Why would Locksmith Joe want to kill everyone else?'

'Because he killed Auntie Gwen. He's a

madman. Uncle Christie testified against him. He escaped so he could do away with us. He's followed them here.'

James crossed his legs and studied the seam in his trousers. 'Were you happy to see Calvin again?'

She flinched. A small reaction and, if he'd blinked, he'd have missed it, but it was there. He'd hit a nerve and he sensed Beth had seen it too.

'Lucy,' Beth said, 'the last few days aside, when was the last time you saw Calvin?'

The young woman shrugged. 'Oh, I don't know, a few weeks before he left for India, I suppose. Why?'

'He's not been in correspondence with you at all?'

'No. Well, he sends his mail to Boyd but I just pass that on. I don't open it.' She fiddled with her fingers. 'Why would he write to me?'

'What about recently?' James said. 'Did you meet up a couple of weeks ago?'

Lucy's fists tightened. 'Whatever do you mean? Calvin wasn't even here two weeks ago.' She sat up straight. 'What's this all about? Why are you bothering me about Calvin? Locksmith Joe is the killer. Why are you bothering us? I thought you were supposed to be helping us.'

'When he arrived at the house last week, you seemed surprised.'

Lucy gawped at James. 'I suppose I was surprised. I got my days mixed up — I thought he was coming later.'

'Did you recognise Calvin?'

She fiddled with her hair. 'Of course. I mean, he's a man now, but you don't forget someone's features, do you?' She checked her watch. 'I should really be getting back to work.'

'What about Josh?' asked Beth.

Lucy swallowed nervously. Her answer was barely audible. 'What about him?'

'Oh come on, Lucy,' James said, 'you know that chap's not Calvin. That's Josh staying at Cory House, isn't it?'

'No!'

'Josh is masquerading as Calvin because your cousin is seriously ill in Bombay. When did you find out?'

'What? I didn't find anything out.' She scrambled for her handbag. 'I really should get back to work.' She made to go.

'Lucy, sit down.'

Beth dragged her chair closer to the girl and held her hand. 'Lucy, if you know this is true, you must speak out. Two murders have taken place and — '

The young woman spluttered. 'No.'

' . . . and, if you're keeping information back from the police, you could go to prison. And then what will happen to Boyd and Suzie?'

Lucy blinked back her tears. She accepted a handkerchief and dabbed her eyes. James reached inside his jacket for his cigarette case and offered one to her. She took it and moved forward for him to light it.

After lighting his own, he said: 'Lucy, no one can blame you for wanting to keep things secret or to help someone, especially if this is family. I'm sure that all of you had the best of intentions, but did you anticipate murder in the proceedings?'

After what felt like an eternity, Lucy slowly shook her head. 'I didn't realise that it would come to this. This wasn't in the plan.' Her eyes pleaded. 'Calvin thinks the world of Boyd, he always has done — he just wanted him to be free.' She blew her nose and continued. 'We're not sure whether Calvin is going to make it or not. He wanted to see Boyd. Boyd's last letter to Cal said that things were even worse since they'd moved from Yorkshire. Uncle Christie only let him out for meal times. Nothing mattered except that house. He was obsessed with it. He was paying to have people to do it up so that it was perfect. That's all he was interested in. It was horrible. He treated Boyd like a piece of rubbish.'

'So Calvin and Josh implemented a plan?'

She appeared resigned. 'They'd planned to kidnap Boyd. Calvin placed an international call to me and asked that I get a passport for him. That was all I had to do; just fill out a few forms and get a photograph done. Boyd explored the house. He knew about the secret passage because Auntie Gwen had researched its history and described the house to him. They used to pretend they had one in the house in Otley. I told Calvin about it — not for any ulterior motive. We just thought it was funny because we knew that Boyd could come and go and had gained more freedom.'

'And he told Josh about it.'

'I presume so.' She brushed her hair back. 'Josh took over all of the preparations.'

'So you knew it was Josh that had arrived, not Calvin.'

'But Josh couldn't have killed Uncle Christie. He didn't arrive until after he'd died. He gave me his itinerary. It was Locksmith Joe. Josh and Calvin are not murderers.' She broke down.

Mr Smythe entered and, on seeing Lucy's distress, faltered. 'Oh, ah, sorry to bother you, Lord Harrington, but there's a Detective Chief Inspector Lane on the telephone.'

'How on earth did he know I was here?'

Beth shrugged and suggested he go find out. He left her to sympathise with Lucy and followed Smythe to a spare desk, where the office manager gave him the receiver.

'Hello, George, what detection skills did you put into play to trace me?'

'I didn't,' replied George. 'The Merryweathers were worried you were going to get yourself into trouble and gave me a heads-up. What's going on?'

James went through his recent exchange with Lucy. 'She's a pawn in the game, as far as I can tell. But she's adamant that she didn't realise murder was on the cards and she's also adamant that Josh didn't arrive until after Christie's death.'

'Ah-ha. Well, we can put that one to bed straight away. Stephen told me about your contact, Ronnie Pickering, so I got on to him. Helpful chap. His contact in Bombay checked through the passenger lists for all Bombay to Delhi flights this month.'

'And?'

'Josh Stirling boarded a flight from Bombay, final destination London, on 10th September. Calvin Christie allegedly checked on to a flight from Bombay on the 19th but never travelled.'

'How on earth did he do that? I thought he was ill?'

'He is. I've checked with the hospital and he's there. I've got to assume that someone else over there did them a favour.'

'Perhaps Josh's cousin, Alastair?'

'Perhaps. The hospital has diagnosed malaria and dysentery.'

'Oh Lord. Are you going over to arrest Josh now?'

'That's partly why I'm calling.'

'Oh?'

'Josh Stirling and Boyd Cameron have disappeared.'

26

'We've put alerts out to airports and shipping lines,' said George. 'I'm guessing they're trying to get back to India. D'you have any idea where they may have gone?'

'Have you asked Ronnie Pickering if he can check the passenger lists for today?'

'Yes. He's getting back to me. Josh thinks things through, so I'm not certain he's going to make it easy for us to find him.'

James clicked his fingers in inspiration. 'Shoreham.'

'What?'

'Shoreham airport. He flew in to Shoreham. He mentioned something to me about knowing people with aircraft down there. They do flights across to France. I'll bet you a pound he's on his way there to pick up a flight to Paris.'

'Right. I'm at Hove police station. I suppose I can't tell you to keep your nose out?'

James discreetly brushed over the question and said he'd meet George at Shoreham. 'You may want to send a constable here. Lucy knows a little more than she originally told you.'

The telephone went dead. James dashed back to the office, picked up Beth's handbag and handed it to her.

'We're off to Shoreham.' He pulled Lucy up from her chair. 'Lucy, if there's anything else you're holding back, now is the time to tell the police. They're on their way here and I would suggest you speak with them. If you refuse, you'll find yourself in far more trouble than you are already.' He opened the door for Beth. 'Come along, darling.'

The road leading to Shoreham airport gave them a good view of the aerodrome. Built in the 1930s, the terminal building was a wonderful example of Art Deco architecture. The walls were pure white with curved corners and a low level flat roof. A number of planes were parked in a line along the verge and one larger aircraft was revving its engines, ready to speed down the grass runway.

'Oh sweetie, I hope that's not the plane they're on.'

James steered the car through the gates and parked close to the terminal entrance. 'If it is, let's hope George can alert the authorities in Paris and persuade them to meet the plane.'

Getting out of his car, James saw two other cars heading for the airport. He guessed this was George and a back-up police presence. He nudged Beth and they scurried across the car park and into the terminal building. It covered an area only half the size of a tennis court. A couple of desks were open and they scanned the destination names and adverts for exotic climes.

Beth grabbed him. 'There. A flight to Paris leaving in fifty minutes. D'you think that's the one?'

'Let's ask.' James greeted the ground stewardess behind the desk. 'I say, I have a couple of friends on the Paris flight and I've something that I need to give to them. Have they checked in yet?'

As soon as he gave the names, the agent nodded. 'Yes, they came through about half an hour ago. They're through those doors there, in the café.'

'Splendid.'

He started to go, but Beth pulled him back. 'What if he's armed or something?' she whispered.

'I can't let him get on that plane, Beth.'

George strode in; a little worse the wear for running. 'Is he here?'

'Yes,' replied James. 'George, let me speak to him. You said yourself he's clever. He may open up to me more than you.'

George scrutinised him. He called across to the agent, showed his credentials and asked if there was another way into the café.

'You can come round the back of the desks here,' the agent said. 'If you follow the corridor, the door to the right leads into the back of the café.' She noticed the two constables waiting outside. 'Is there going to be trouble?'

'Nothing for you to worry about,' said George. 'We are probably going to have to take a couple of your passengers off the Paris flight.'

She regarded James. 'The two you mentioned?'

'Yes.'

George poked James in the chest. 'Go and talk to him. Keep him chatting and steer him to some sort of confession. We haven't actually got one iota of evidence yet.' He started to go but turned back. 'Oh yes, and no heroics.'

George followed the agent through a doorway behind the desks.

'Come along, darling' said Beth. 'Let's do this. If nothing else, I can be there for Boyd.'

He groaned. 'Oh Lord, poor Boyd. Do you think he even knows that that's not Calvin in there?'

He opened the ornate swing doors and they entered the tiny departure lounge. Around fifteen tables and cushioned chairs were dotted about and waitresses in black dresses with white aprons busied themselves. Crockery chinked and travellers chatted quietly with one another. James dipped his head to a table at the far end. The two brothers sat with their drinks looking across the airfield. He couldn't help but feel a twinge of remorse. Josh was pointing to the different aircraft and telling the young boy what type of plane each was and where it would be going to.

A huge part of James wanted to let them go; let Boyd be with his brother, a man he'd built up to be his hero during his early years. He was only a few minutes away from that dream. His excitement must be beyond belief. But here he stood about to snatch that dream away. Beth tugged his sleeve.

'Are you all right, sweetie?'

He patted her hand. This was going to be difficult. A door on the far side of the lounge edged open. George hovered before heading toward a nearby table to wait for James to make his move.

'Yes, darling, I'm fine. Let's get this over with.'

He steered Beth toward Josh's table. Josh, aware of movement behind him, glanced over his shoulder. James noted the flash of horror on his face, which turned to surprise.

He leapt up. 'Ah, Boyd, look who's

come to see us off.'

James squeezed Boyd's shoulder. The boy's pink eyes sparkled with joy. He wore a smart linen suit purchased, James guessed, especially for the journey. Josh remained calm and invited them to sit. They ordered tea.

Beth reached for Boyd's hand. 'Boyd, I've been to this airport a few times. I happen to know someone in the control room. Would you like to see it?'

'Yes please,' said Boyd who sought permission from Josh to do so. Josh shifted in his seat and checked his watch. 'Our flight leaves soon.'

'Oh, we won't be long. If you'd rather we didn't . . . '

Josh waved a hand at them and told Boyd to make the most of it. James glimpsed beyond Josh to see George take a seat at the table immediately behind. The young man sipped his tea.

'How did you know I was here?'

James relaxed back in his chair. 'You mentioned Shoreham during a chat we had when you first arrived. It seemed like the obvious place. I heard you'd gone. I got the impression that an ocean trip wasn't on the cards and that you wanted to return to India with the utmost urgency.'

'You're right. I'm leaving Lucy to tie up the loose ends of the estate. I know that my father has left us a fortune, so we're selling the house and splitting the profits between us.'

'Have you let the police know you're leaving? There are still two murders being investigated. I'm surprised they're letting you leave.'

Josh laughed. 'But that's nothing to do with me. That's Locksmith Joe.'

'Come, come, Calvin,' said James. 'Do you think we're all that naive?'

Josh stared at his hands then pushed his cup and saucer away. 'Why are you here, Lord Harrington?'

'I think you know why.'

'I came here to get my brother and take him back with me. It's what we've planned all along. I can't help it if it coincides with murder. Boyd is best off with me and away from all of this. You can't blame me for that, can you?'

'Not at all. I believe it was planned. But things changed, didn't they?'

The young man gazed out of the window. He scanned the pale autumn sky and tears welled up.

'Josh?'

Josh reacted to his name and closed his eyes in realisation. 'How much do you know?'

'I know that, originally, the plan was just as you said. Calvin and you would build the business up and get enough funds for Calvin to come and get Boyd and take him back to Bombay. I know that Calvin is seriously ill.'

Josh's bottom lip trembled.

'I know that's when your plans changed. That's when you began typing the letters to Boyd, isn't it?'

He brushed a tear away. 'Calvin was overwrought. He may die and he didn't want to die without seeing Boyd. He just wanted a few hours with Boyd. We'd saved enough to do all of that and get him back here after . . .'

'After Calvin's death.'

A nod. 'When Boyd mentioned in his

letters that things were worse for him in Cavendish, Calvin looked like a man defeated.' Josh made a fist. 'I had to do something. I couldn't let Calvin die without seeing Boyd. I said I'd do anything — ' He checked himself.

James smiled. 'You said you'd do anything for Calvin because you would do anything for love.' He reached inside his pocket and brought out the page of the letter he'd found on the staircase. He slid it across. 'Love is a powerful thing, Josh.'

Josh closed his eyes and James sensed that a wave of relief had washed through the young man. A great burden, this forbidden love, was no longer a secret. Josh brushed another tear away. The waitress approached the table but James advised her that they needed nothing. He dragged his chair closer to Josh. George edged his own seat further forward.

'You arrived on an earlier flight and lay low,' said James quietly. 'You hung around the house, put extra sleeping draughts in Christie's milk and, I'm guessing, went to his room via the secret passage to finish him off. It didn't take much effort because he was so drugged. The following day, I believe it was you at the scarecrow festival. Am I right?'

The young man nodded. 'I'd heard about Locksmith Joe being free — that played straight into my hands. I strangled Christie to set up Joe. I slipped a note through the door at Cory House; arranged to meet Jeannie in the village. I kept those overcoats on, messed myself up a bit to look like him. I got some spirit glue and stuck a beard on. I thought I was quite convincing.'

'You arranged to meet Jeannie in the village and, dressed as Locksmith Joe, you strangled her.'

George joined them at the table.

Josh closed his eyes. 'Oh God, what a mess. What a ruddy mess.' He put his head in his hands.

George quietly cautioned him. 'Don't think about running.'

'I can't imagine you're here on your own, Inspector. Besides, I don't want to upset Boyd.'

An announcement came for passengers to board the Paris flight. James searched for Beth and saw her at another table with Boyd. She sat close to the boy and was speaking quietly. The young lad had tears streaming down his cheeks. James felt like crying himself. She was telling him he wouldn't be getting on the plane. His heart went out to her. What a sad state of affairs. So much love, so much hope and good intentions.

'Josh, why did you not just ask to adopt Boyd?'

Josh's eyes were fierce. It was the same glare that James had seen at the scarecrow festival; the same fierceness he'd seen on meeting him at Cory House when he'd spoken about Christie.

'If you saw how much hurt and anger that man Christie and his sister caused, you wouldn't need to ask. The man wasn't just cruel — he was a domestic tyrant. How the hell was Calvin going to be able to adopt Boyd from his own father? He inflicted emotional abuse if they didn't play by the rules. But, apart from a knife attack, he had no proof. And Christie made sure that the nurse treating Cal wasn't going to talk. He threatened anyone who could make life difficult for him. Christ! What sort of man does that? Jeannie was as bad. She treated Boyd like he was something she'd scraped off her shoe.'

James admitted that he knew about the knife attack and that, had Josh refused to confess he wasn't Calvin, the lack of a scar would prove it. The young man's defeated smile told him what he needed to know.

'What you won't know is that, had Calvin been able to relive that moment, he would have killed his father there and then. He wanted him dead for everything he inflicted on the family. On Boyd and his mother. An eye for an eye.' Josh met James' gaze. 'So that's what I did.'

He scanned the lounge and spotted Boyd. His expression softened. 'Lord Harrington, I have no right to ask, but can you get a message to Calvin and tell him I'm sorry? And Lucy. I think she knew who I was but she didn't let on. She did nothing wrong; she just got Boyd a passport. Is there any way you can get Boyd across to India? I've messed up on all fronts. I don't want to mess up on what we originally planned.'

James wanted to help Boyd. He'd clearly had an awful start in life and it would do him good to see his brother. 'Josh, I will do my best to fulfil your original wishes. As for Calvin, I think it best that you write a letter and Boyd can deliver it for you. I don't profess to agree with the relationship you have, but a letter is something he can always read. Words from a stranger mean very little.'

Josh's face was distraught as he rose wearily from his chair. Passengers began making their way onto the airfield. As Josh stood up, Boyd raced across the lounge and hugged him tight. Josh kissed the top of his head.

'It's all right, Boyd. You'll be fine, I promise.'

'But where will I go? I'll not see Calvin, will I?' As fast as he wiped the tears, more came.

Passengers, readying themselves to walk out to the plane, stared as they went by. Boyd couldn't catch his breath he was so distraught.

James stood behind Boyd, drew him close and placed his hands on his shoulders as he watched George escort Josh away. The man didn't stand a chance in the dock and would surely either hang or spend the rest of his life in prison.

Beth joined him. 'I thought he might run.'

'I don't think he has anything to run for, darling.' He turned Boyd. His pink eyes were red-rimmed and he began to shiver. James took his jacket off and wrapped it around the boy's shoulders. He simply couldn't begin to comprehend what the lad must be thinking. He sat Boyd down and pulled a chair across to sit opposite him.

'Josh has asked that I do everything I can to get you across to see Calvin, and I promised I would. You may not be travelling on an aircraft right now, but I will do my utmost to make sure you travel on one in the next couple of days.'

Boyd gazed at him and then through the glass doors to see Josh being led away. His gaze never shifted until Josh was out of sight.

27

The stone-built barn at the back of the Half Moon buzzed as villagers mingled back and forth. Bales of hay, deckchairs, school canteen tables and some wooden benches from the pub made up the make-shift seating. A queue of residents and farmers snaked along the wall, each waiting to pick up a portion of the harvest supper. Graham Porter, along with several farmers, had laid out a row of platters of roasted goose stuffed with vegetables and apples, followed by huge slabs of gammon boiled in cider. He placed a selection of food onto the plates. His wife, Sarah, ladled on an accompanying portion of pease pudding, a traditional British dish consisting of mashed split peas, onion and carrot.

At the end of the line, James, in his role as the Lord of the Harvest, distributed the traditional harvest bread moulded into the shape of a wheatsheaf. He tore pieces off for each villager. As the last of them went along the line, James picked up a plate to receive his own meal. He breathed in the smell of succulent meat juices. The goose was cooked to perfection. The gammon fell apart and the pease pudding was firm, yet fluffy. He remembered his grandfather speaking of the small village of Pease Pottage, a few miles up the road. Rumour had it that the village got its name from serving this dish to convicts in transit to London.

Donovan and Kate stood further along and handed out small tots of Harvest Gold ale. The villagers and farmers took their seats with their meals and drinks and the noise levels rose.

With Beth following behind, James found his way to a long bench where he was to preside as Lord of the Harvest. On either side of them were Stephen, Anne, GJ and Catherine. James stood and rang a large cowbell to quieten everyone down.

'Do carry on eating. Before I ask Stephen to ask for a blessing on us this evening, I wanted to share some good news with you all.'

A murmur went through the barn.

'As you know, a young man arrived at our old stables back in the spring and, thanks to some detective work and good luck, we were able to help him move on from his homeless existence. GJ here has since opened up a thriving art studio at Harrington's and you'll see that he's had this rather lovely lady in tow all summer.'

James paused as a few suggestive comments were uttered by the farmers. He cleared his throat.

'To get to the point, I'm honoured to announce the engagement of GJ and Catherine.' A huge cheer rang around the barn and James had to ring the cowbell again to quieten everyone. 'The wedding will be on the first of December here at St Nicholas' church.' He raised a glass. 'Please raise your glasses. Congratulations, GJ and Catherine!'

'Congratulations!' everyone chorused.

Stephen, looking more like a cowboy than a vicar, in his checked shirt and blue jeans, took over and asked that they remain silent for a short prayer.

'Lord, we ask that you bless this food that you bring to our table and join us in celebrating this harvest s-supper. We thank you for providing our farmers with the tools and skills to b-bring the harvest in and allow us the pleasure of enjoying this feast. Amen.'

Bert, who sat alongside Donovan, shouted, 'Nice and short, vicar, that's what we like!'

A chuckle went round the barn; Stephen took his seat next to James.

'W-what a wonderful turnout.'

'Isn't it. Out of all the festivals we celebrate through the year, I think this one brings more villagers out than any of them. I honestly believe the whole village is here.'

Beth closed her eyes in delight. 'This food is delicious.'

Anne announced that she'd already asked Graham for the gammon in cider recipe. Beth asked that she make a copy for her too.

'S-so, is everything wrapped up with this C-Cameron business?' asked Stephen.

'More or less, yes. George got a straight confession from Josh. He knew things had gone horribly wrong. The police aren't fools and were already piecing together the flight details, or lack of them. Lucy, I believe, may be charged. She knew a lot more than she led us to believe. She certainly should have come forward sooner.'

'Did you ever l-learn why Boyd sent you the letters?'

James said he was an astute young man. 'He'd seen the difference in the spelling of Calvin's alleged wife and he heard movement in the passage the night Christie was killed. He sent the letters to me so they wouldn't be found. I think he thought it was Calvin and he was trying to protect him. He trusted me. Unfortunately, I abused that trust.'

Anne reminded him that, if he hadn't, a murderer would have gone free. James thanked her for her words, but suggested that the net had been closing in even at that point.

'There were a couple of things, in hindsight, that now make sense,' said James. 'When we met Lucy at Elsie's, she seemed overly worried about where the letters were. Although she hadn't read them, she was worried about what was written in them. And when I announced to the others that Calvin had arrived, there was anxiety written all over his face. I now know that this was the moment of truth. If Boyd didn't recognise Josh as Calvin, his cover would be blown. I'm still not sure whether Lucy recognised him. And, of course, when we went to hunt for the secret passage, he was careful to ensure that I searched an area well away from where the passage really was.'

'Oh d-dear. What a t-tangled web we weave,' said Stephen.

'When first we practise to deceive,' added Anne. 'And he didn't put up a fight.'

'No, and Calvin's prognosis isn't good. He's been struck down by two serious illnesses. Josh has done what he set out to do.'

'A-and did Calvin ever m-marry?'

'No. It appears this Jayne girl was part of their crowd. He made all that up to get the inheritance.'

'I thought it might be Suzie who was the killer,' Anne said. 'She just seemed too sure of herself.'

Stephen groaned at his wife's logic and turned his attention to James. 'A-and Boyd?'

James put his knife and fork down. 'Ah, well, that was one piece of good news. Kushal has taken Boyd under his wing and they are in Bombay as we speak. Kushal has arranged for Calvin to be taken to a better hospital and has promised to update me once he has news.'

'Sweetie,' said Beth, 'if Calvin recovers, will he be charged with anything?'

'I wouldn't imagine so. George said he doesn't really have any tangible proof. The statement Josh signed indicates that the plan was his; he's not incriminated Calvin at all.'

Bert raised a glass and called across. 'Nice nosh.'

James held his own glass up. He scooped the rest of his pease pudding up and savoured the last morsel of gammon. After dabbing his lips with a napkin, he pushed his plate away.

Stephen turned quickly as if he'd just remembered something. 'W-what about Locksmith Joe?'

James was aware that both Beth and

Anne were keen for an update but all he could give them was a helpless shrug.

'He'll have to give himself up. We searched every nook and cranny in that house for a camera. We found one, but there was no film in it. Boyd searched his room, too, but he says he never saw it. Cameron must have thrown it all out when they moved.'

Stephen frowned and looked at Anne. 'Have you asked Luke and Mark? D-did they take anything from that r-rubbish tip? I know the pair of them went through it along with a few others.'

'I told them they weren't to take anything but I know they all did,' said Anne. She shivered. 'Typical boys messing about in a place that's filthy and probably full of germs.'

Stephen sought out their two boys, who raced across from the small play area that had been set up for the children.

'Luke, M-Mark, that rubbish tip at the back of Cory House. Did you t-take anything?'

The boys remained quiet but the rising colour in their faces gave them away.

'Y-you know you should always ask p-permission before taking things, don't you?'

'But it was rubbish,' said Luke.

'And it wasn't just us that took things,' Mark added, his bottom lip protruding.

James squatted down. 'How would you like to solve a mystery?'

Their eyes lit up.

'Among those things you took, was there a camera?'

'It's a rusty old thing. I've got it in my cupboard. Have I got to give it back?' Luke said.

'Is it going to solve a murder?' asked Mark excitedly.

James felt an adrenalin rush. 'Do you know, Mark, I think it may well do.' He turned to Stephen. 'Can you nip across the green with the boys and find it?'

Anne, not wanting to miss out, said that she, Stephen and the boys would go and hunt down the camera. Within a minute, they'd gone.

Beth got up. 'Mr Chrichton is over there. Shall I ask if we can make use of his dark room?'

'Good idea. You do that and I'd best get on and announce the distribution of the cake.'

He sought out Rose and Lilac Crumb who were already levering off the lids to several cake tins. Inside were home-made caraway cakes. The smell of freshly-baked sponge overwhelmed him.

'I say, ladies, these look wonderful and smell delicious.'

'Took us all weekend to cook,' said Lilac.

'A real treat for everyone,' her sister put in.

'Are you announcing it?'

'Don't want 'em going stale.'

Without further ado, James picked up the cowbell and rang it. The room hushed.

'Ladies, gentleman and children. In keeping with the tradition of the harvest supper, Rose and Lilac Crumb have baked this year's caraway cake.' He breathed in the aroma. 'I have to say, this may be one of the best we've tasted. Once you're ready, come and get a piece. We'll then clear the floor a little and Bob Tanner will be leading a barn dance.'

The noise levels rose again as villagers scrambled to queue for cake. The ladies of the WI sorted out tea and coffee and a number of men began clearing bales of hay to one side to allow room for dancing. Beth negotiated her way through the crowds to join him.

'Mr Chrichton is more than happy to develop the film. He can do it now, if it's urgent.'

James brushed her hair from her eyes. 'I hope and pray that this is the camera we're seeking.'

Beth agreed and commented that Bert would also be pleased to have this particular event cleared up. Luke hurtled up to him and held out a dirty, dusty camera.

Chrichton joined them. 'Is that the one?'

James turned the camera over in his hand; a wide grin on seeing the make: Exakta. 'This is the one! Are you all right to do this now? It is harvest supper, after all.'

'I've had my meal,' replied Chrichton. 'I'm not too fussed about dancing. You stay here and do your Lord of the Harvest duties. I'll be back as soon as I can.'

They watched him go. James felt like the proverbial cat on a hot tin roof. He wished he had patience during times like this and forced himself to calm down.

'Well,' he said to Beth and the Merryweathers, 'there's nothing we can do now until that film's developed. Let's have some caraway cake and take our mind off of things.'

The caraway cake, though, did nothing to distract James from thinking about the film. He watched as Bert shared a joke with Charlie Hawkins and his children. If that film did not provide the evidence Locksmith Joe sought, the escaped convict would have to give himself up. Bert rode his luck at times and the longer he sheltered a convict, the more trouble he was likely to be in. He didn't like to think of his old friend being charged for harbouring a criminal.

George interrupted his thoughts.

'Ah, hello, George. I didn't think you would make it.'

His friend shrugged his raincoat off and

put it over the back of a chair. 'Don't like to miss out on these unless I have to.'

'Any news?'

'Yes, some of it good. Josh is under lock and key. Lucy's been cautioned. I gave her a telling-off about holding information back.'

'I get the feeling that Lucy is a law-abiding citizen.'

'She was shaking like a leaf when I spoke with her. I don't think she'll be breaking the law again.' His expression brightened. 'And Mr Patel called. It appears that, on seeing Boyd, Calvin has taken a turn for the better. They're not promising anything yet, but it seems his affection for the boy, and the new hospital he's in, have perked him up.'

'That is good news,' said James, 'although I'm sure Calvin will be heartbroken over what happened with Josh. Listen, Donovan has the harvest tot over there. I think you probably deserve a couple, so why don't you relax and forget about today's activities?'

George thanked him and said that he would do just that. He waved hello to

Beth and made his way to the WI table to see what was left to eat and drink.

Beth dragged James away and they joined in a couple of dances. Breathless after an energetic reel, James checked his watch and found himself repeatedly looking at the door. Time dragged terribly when one was waiting for urgent news. It was like waiting for the twins to be born all over again. He'd never forget that day; the matron had ordered him to sit down while the midwife and the nurses rushed here and there. He remembered a clock on the wall opposite where he had watched the second hand tick, ever so slowly. Sometimes, it had felt as if it were going backward. After what seemed like an eternity, Harry and Oliver arrived into the world.

The evening drew to a close and, one by one, the villagers gathered their things and said goodbye. Many, the worse for wear on cider and brandy tots, weaved from one side of the pavement to the other, their arms around each other, singing songs about the harvest, cider and farming. The ladies of the WI scurried around with brooms and bins tidying up. The Merryweathers, Donovan, Kate, Bert and the Snoop Sisters all came together to help.

The door opened. James swung round to see Mr Chrichton striding toward him holding out the photographs.

James tugged George's sleeve. 'You're going to want to see these.'

28

James, George, Bert and the Merryweathers huddled in a corner of the stone barn with Mr Chrichton. George chivvied the Snoop Sisters back to their tidying up and Donovan and Kate returned to the pub. After some pleading, the Merryweathers allowed Luke and Mark to stay over with Tommy and Susan Hawkins. They now had the barn to themselves and George, having leafed through some photographs of paintings and antiques, stopped at the last one. James peered over his shoulder.

The black and white shot showed a heavily-built man with his hands around a woman's throat. The woman's eyes bulged and her face appeared flushed as she grabbed at her assailant's hands. Beth, standing the other side of George, shook her head in exasperation.

'But we can't see who that is. How does that prove anything? The man has his back to the camera.' She looked at

Chrichton. 'Were there no more prints?'

'No,' said Chrichton. 'that was the last one used on the film.'

'No, wait!' James snatched the print from George. He prodded it hard. 'See here, here's the proof you need. Look at the reflection. There.'

George ordered everyone to give him some room. 'You'll get your turn. Now, James, what're you looking at?'

'Here, there's a mirror on the back wall. Look at the reflection of the man with the camera.'

George screwed his eyes up and his weary expression turned to one of recognition. 'Locksmith Joe.'

Relief washed over the group. Bert took the picture from James and studied it. A beaming smile lit up his face.

'Told yer, didn't 'e? He told you there was a photo and there it is.'

The argument that followed between James, Bert and George went on for several minutes. George tore James off a strip for leaving him out of the loop; James retaliated, insisting he was put in a tight spot by Bert, who immediately insisted that he did the right thing and that everything came out all right in the wash. Beth, the Merryweathers and Chrichton left them to it and helped with the last of the clearing up.

George jerked his head at Bert. 'You're lucky you weren't caught with him. I'd have had to lock you up, you know that, don't you?'

'Yeah, but you didn't, did yer? It's all worked out well. I can bring Joe in to the station tomorrow.'

'Make sure you do.' George took the photograph back from Bert and turned to go. 'If he's not at Lewes first thing in the morning — '

'Blimey, I said I'd bring 'im and I will.' Bert flashed his annoyance as George walked away. More sheepishly, he turned to James. 'I'm sorry, Jimmy boy. I pu' you in a spot and I don't like myself for doin' it.' He held out his hand.

James took it. 'I'd appreciate it if you didn't jeopardise our friendship again, Bert. Not only did it put us on unfamiliar territory, but I had to keep things from George. There's a line that you simply don't cross and you leapt over it like a gazelle.'

Bert, cap in hand, apologised again and trudged out. He turned at the door with a hopeful gaze. 'We on for a beer tomorrow?'

James grinned. 'Of course.'

Beth wandered across to him and took his hand. 'Everything resolved itself in the end.'

'Yes, our murderer is locked up, our escaped convict will, I'm sure, be released once all the statements have been made. Calvin is making good progress and Lucy has escaped with a caution. Cory House is now on the market. Let's hope the next residents have a better time there.' He kissed her forehead. 'A good job all round, I'd say.'

The barn was almost empty. It was hard to think that, an hour ago, the place had been alive with music, dancing and laughter. Now, the only people here, apart from him and Beth, were the Merryweathers who came toward them with four glasses of sherry on a small tray.

'I-it's all we could find,' said Stephen. 'I

th-think a toast is in order for a-another mystery solved.'

'You're very kind, Stephen. Cheers.' James checked his watch and turned to Anne. 'I say, is it too forward of me to request a hot chocolate at the vicarage?'

No answer was required. The four of them made their way out. James closed the barn door and joined Beth. They followed Stephen and Anne to the vicarage, where Beth reminded them all that Christmas and the wedding would soon be upon them. Anne chuckled.

'Let's hope that one will be mystery-free.'

James allowed himself a brief chuckle. 'Let's hope so indeed.'

THE END

See below for Grandma Harrington's recipes.

Steak and Kidney Mixture (serves 4-6)
This steamed mixture can be served in a pie with puff pastry or in a steamed suet pudding or, as Grandma Harrington sometimes did; simply serve with vegetables and potatoes.

1½ lbs/680g of beef braising steak and kidney (Two thirds steak, one third kidney)
1 onion
Half a dozen mushrooms
Water
1 tbsp gravy powder
1 meat stock cube
A sprinkle of salt and pepper
4 tbsp plain flour

Cut the steak and kidney into cubes; slice the onions and mushrooms.
Put the flour, gravy powder, salt, pepper and crumbled stock cube in a bowl, tip the steak, kidney, onions and mushrooms into that bowl and stir. Ensure that everything is coated evenly with flour.
Grease a suitably-sized pudding bowl

and tip the ingredients in. (Ensure the bowl can fit into a saucepan.)

Add half a cup of water to the ingredients.

Put a large saucepan on the stove and add one inch of water to the bottom.

Seal the pudding bowl tightly and lower this into the saucepan.

Bring the water to the boil and reduce to a simmer.

Simmer for 2-3 hours. (Don't forget to top up the water in the saucepan as it evaporates quickly.)

About half an hour before you're ready to serve, check the dish. If the gravy is too thin for your liking, now is the time to thicken it up.

Caraway Seed Cake

3oz/85g butter
3oz/85g caster sugar
3 eggs
A dash of vanilla extract
4oz/113g plain flour
½ tsp baking powder
1 tbsp milk

Cream the butter.
Add sugar and beat until feather-light.
Whisk the eggs and vanilla extract and slowly add this to the mixture. Do it gradually otherwise it will curdle. (If it begins to curdle, fold in some of the flour.)
Fold in the flour and baking powder.
Add the caraway seeds.
Add a little milk to ensure a 'loaf' consistency.

Grease a small loaf-tin and tip the mixture in.
Add to a pre-heated oven (gas mark 4 or 180° centigrade or 350° Fahrenheit) for 30 minutes.
Allow to cool before removing.

We do hope that you have enjoyed reading this large print book.

Did you know that all of our titles are available for purchase?

We publish a wide range of high quality large print books including:
Romances, Mysteries, Classics
General Fiction
Non Fiction and Westerns

Special interest titles available in large print are:
The Little Oxford Dictionary
Music Book, Song Book
Hymn Book, Service Book

Also available from us courtesy of Oxford University Press:
Young Readers' Dictionary
(large print edition)
Young Readers' Thesaurus
(large print edition)

For further information or a free brochure, please contact us at:
Ulverscroft Large Print Books Ltd.,
The Green, Bradgate Road, Anstey,
Leicester, LE7 7FU, England.
Tel: (00 44) **0116 236 4325**
Fax: (00 44) **0116 234 0205**